IN THE WAR
THE ZONE

An Uncommon
American Love Story

JOHN HENRY BREBBIA

This book is a work of fiction. References to real people, events, establishments, organizations or locales are intended only to provide a sense of
authenticity, and are used fictitiously. All other characters, and all other
incidents and dialogue, are drawn from the author's imagination and are
not to be construed as real.

Acknowledgements
Copy Editor: Trish Brebbia

ISBN: 1466290943

ISBN 13: 9781466290945

CAROL,

I'll be expecting a review.

All the best,

Jack Quinlin

04. 11. 12

*For Trish still my one true love and Anthony and Christian
still the two best sons any man ever had*

By John Henry Brebbia
APO 123

about the author

The author grew up in Brookline, Massachusetts, attended public schools there and went on to Stonehill College and Boston College Law School. He served in the US Army Judge Advocate General's Corps in the USA and in France. After his military service he moved to Washington, D.C. where he was a Trial Attorney at the Federal Trade Commission and then a managing partner at Alston & Bird, a major corporate law firm. He served as a member of the President's Commission on White House Fellowships, before relocating to Las Vegas as president of a bank holding company and vice-chairman of its subsidiary bank. He later became an entrepreneur and private practitioner. Among his civic activities, he was chairman of the Nevada Humanities Committee; vice chairman of the Governor's Advisory Council on Education Relating to the Holocaust; a member of the boards of the Nevada Commission on Cultural Affairs, public radio station KNPR and the Federation of State Humanities Councils. Currently, he serves as general counsel and a board member of an Irish technology company. For the past 25 years, he has been a member of Lefty Salazar & Associates, a Las Vegas writer's group whose members have published a number of works of fiction and non-fiction. His first novel – *APO 123* – was published in 2010.

A man said to the universe:
"Sir, I exist!"
"However," replied the universe.
"The fact has not created in me
A sense of obligation."

Stephen Crane

glossary of nautical terms

Aft – the rear or stern end of a vessel

Anchor – object intended to prevent or slow the drift of a vessel

Anchor rode – the anchor line, rope or cable connecting the anchor chain to the vessel

Barometer – an instrument for measuring atmospheric pressure and thus forecasting weather

Bitter end – the last part or loose end of a rope or cable

Boom vang – line used to pull down the boom

Bowsprit – a spar projecting from the bow used as an anchor for the forestay and other rigging

Bulkhead – vertical surface or wall within the hull of a ship

Cabin – an enclosed room aboard a vessel where passengers and members of the crew sleep

Cabin top – top of the cabin on deck

Catwalk – the narrow walkway of a dock used to moor motorized boats or sailboats

Cleat – a stationary device used to secure a rope aboard a vessel or on a dock

Cockpit – the open area towards the stern of a small-decked vessel that houses the rudder controls

Cockpit dodger – a hood forward of the cockpit to protect the crew from wind and spray

Coffee grinder – slang term for a winch with opposing double handles used on racing vessels to quickly haul in sheets

Companionway – a raised hatchway (entrance) in the vessel's deck, with a ladder leading below

Companionway hatch – the hooded entrance-hatch to the main cabins

Cordage – ropes in the rigging of a vessel

Cringle – metal ring at the corner of a sail to which a line is attached

Cutter – a single-masted vessel, fore-and-aft rigged, with two or more headsails and often a bowsprit

Davit – device for hoisting and lowering a boat, such as a dingy

Deck – permanent covering over a compartment or hull of a ship (vessel)

Dingy – a small open boat often used as a tender for a larger vessel

Dingy garage – a compartment for storing a dingy

Double lifelines – double lines running along the outside of the deck attached to stanchions, creating railings around the edges of a vessel

Double reef - to make the mainsail smaller by lowering the sail to the second set of reef points and then tying off or securing the slack part of the sail to the boom using the second set of reef points, usually to guard against adverse effects of strong wind or to slow the vessel

Drogue – a device (sea anchor) to slow down a vessel in a storm so that it does not speed excessively down the slope of a wave and crash into the next one

Escutcheon – part of a vessel's stern where the name is displayed

Fenders – cylindrical air filled plastic or rubber bumpers hung off the side of a vessel or dock to prevent damage to the dock and vessel

Force 10 winds – a storm with whole gale force winds registering 10 on the Beaufort scale (less than in a hurricane)

Foresail – the triangular sale hung to the forestay of a cutter or sloop

Forward – towards the bow of the vessel

Forward cabin – cabin located towards the bow of a vessel

Forward hatch - a covered opening in a vessel's deck located towards the bow of the vessel through which access is made to the lower deck

Fluttering the sails – causing them to flap rapidly when headed into the wind or when pulled closer to the center of the vessel

Galley – the kitchen of a vessel

Grab rails – Handhold fittings mounted on the cabin tops and sides of a vessel for personal safety while moving around the vessel

Halyard – a line used to raise and lower the head of any sail

Harness rings – rings on a safety harness used to tighten the straps

Hatch – a covered opening in a vessel's deck through which access is made to the lower deck

Head – the toilet or latrine of a vessel

Headsail – any sail flown in front of the most forward mast

Head-to-wind – the bow of the vessel is pointed directly into the wind

Heaving-to – slowing or stopping the forward motion of a sailing vessel by lashing the helm, turning the rudder hard into the wind

Heeling over – leaning or healing over caused by wind pressure on the sails

Helm – the wheel

Jack wire – the line from the bow to the stern on both port and starboard used to clip on the safety harness to secure the crew to the vessel while giving them the freedom to walk on the deck

Jibing – zig-zagging with the stern of the vessel so as to travel upwind faster

Knot – a unit of speed: one nautical mile (1.51 miles) per hour

Leech end – aft or trailing edge of a fore-and-aft sail; the leeward edge of a spinnaker

Leeward – in the direction that the wind is blowing towards; the downwind side

Life jacket – an inflatable jacket that keeps a person afloat in the water

Lifeline stanchion - a vertical post near a deck's edge that supports the lifelines (railings) around the edges of a vessel

Lifelines – lines running along the outside of the deck attached to stanchions, creating railings around the edges of a vessel

Lower deck – deck immediately over the hold of a vessel with two decks

Luff – the forward edge of a sail

Luff cringle - metal ring at the forward edge of a sail to which a line is attached

Mainsail – the sail that is located aft of the mast

Mainsail halyard - a line used to raise and lower the head of the mainsail

Pier – a loading platform extending at an angle from the shore

Performance cruiser – a sailing vessel whose stiffness is derived from a lower center of gravity and a with a displacement/length ratio of 55 to 339

Port – the left hand side of a boat looking forward

Port lights – red lights on the left hand side of the vessel

Port locker – locker on the left hand side of a vessel

Port side deck – deck on the left hand side of a vessel

Pulpit – an area enclosed by a metal railing located at the bow of the vessel

Pushpit – an area enclosed by a metal railing located at the stern of the boat

Reef – to make the mainsail smaller by lowering the sail to specific reef points and then tying off or securing the slack part of the sail to the boom using the reef points, usually to guard against adverse effects of strong wind or to slow the vessel

Rode – a chain, rope or cable attached to the anchor (anchor line)

Safety harness – a harness with a tether line that snaps onto secure fixtures on the deck to prevent crew members from falling overboard, especially in stormy seas

Sailing vessel – a large wind-powered vessel (yacht)

Sheet – a rope used to control how far out the sail goes; the main control line

Skipper – the captain of a ship

Slicker – a waterproof jacket made of plastic or rubber that protects a seaman from the cold and wet

Snap hook – a spring loaded metal fitting

Sou'wester – a storm from the southwest; a type of waterproof hat with a wide brim over the neck, worn in storms

Spinnaker – a large sail flown in front of the vessel while heading downwind

Stanchion – an upright metal post near a deck's edge that holds the lifelines (railings) in place

Starboard – when facing forward, the right side of the vessel

Starboard chock – wooden wedge on the right side of the vessel used to secure moving objects on deck

Stay – a large strong rope or wire that supports the mast in a direct line from the mast to the bow of a vessel

Staysail – an auxiliary sail, often triangular, set on a stay instead of a mast

Stern – back part of a vessel

Stern line – a docking line leading from the stern of a vessel

Stern rail – railing at the back part of a vessel

Tack – steering the bow of a sailing vessel through the wind; forward lower corner of a sail, where the luff and the foot meet

Tacking – zig-zagging with the bow of the vessel so as to travel upwind faster

Tacking and jibing – zig-zagging alternately with the bow and the stern of the vessel

Tack hook – hook on the lower corner of a sail

Tether – a line that connects a person's safety harness to a secure part of the vessel like the jack wires

Toe rail – a low strip running around the edge of the deck like a low bulwark

Topping lift – an adjustable line from the mast to support the aft end of the boom and to support it when the mainsail is lowered or is being reefed, preventing it from falling into the cockpit

Transom – more or less flat surface across the stern of a vessel

Transom ladder – a ladder extending from the stern of the vessel used for boarding

Traveler – a piece of hardware that generally runs on a track secured to the deck or cabin top allowing for the adjustment of where the mainsheet comes back to the cockpit

Vessel – a yacht

Weatherfax – marine weather forecast transmitted by e-mail from the National Weather Service

Wheel – a wheel with a horizontal axis, connected by cables to the rudder

Winch – a drum type mechanical device with gears used to pull lines in when a significant amount of force is on the line

Windward – the upwind side of a vessel

Yankee – a fore-sail flying above and forward of the jib.

chapter

1

Gibb Quinn stepped down off the first train he'd ever boarded—an Amtrak coach out of Penn Station—and faced into an East wind blowing hard off Long Island Sound. Swirling leaves dusted the bare empty platform, in the darkness devoid of their autumn brilliance. Tim Perkins had warned him that in places like Chatham, Connecticut the temperature could turn cold without any advance notice. Not at all like Seattle where Gibb had just departed from and where the weather in September was so predictable. New England weather was the one subject his college roommate had gained any useful knowledge of during the four years he had wasted at Exeter Academy, and thus the only thing for certain Gibb knew about this subject. It would have been different, had Gibb not made a habit of changing channels whenever the local TV weathermen switched to forecasting the weather in other parts of the country, certain as he had been that this information would never be of any practical use to him.

Tim Perkins was the one who rescued him from the apartment near the area in Vegas known as *the Strip* where he'd been hiding out for the longest time. Had Tim chosen not to intervene, Gibb might still be stuck there, swilling vodka and mourning his mother and feeling sorry for himself. Rich as Tim's family was, it never mattered to Tim that his best friend was raised in a run-down trailer park on the fringes of the black ghetto in Vegas. The black ghetto was called Westside. The gangbanger neighborhood bordering it where the trailer park was located didn't rate a formal name. Metro cops called it *the war zone.* This was name enough for Gibb and his friends.

Gibb started towards the worn iron staircase leading to a dimly lit asphalt parking lot below the station. Without warning, an icy blast penetrated his rib cage, stopping him in his tracks. He dropped his duffel bag on the platform—laid his carryall on top of it— and zipped his windbreaker all the way up. Without thinking, he checked the rolls of dimes stored in the side pockets of his windbreaker. The feel of the rolls of dimes brought his thoughts back around to Vegas.

What troubled Gibb the most was not being able to rescue his mother from that lousy house trailer before she died of cancer. She hadn't lived long enough to collect a dollar's worth of pay-back for yanking him out of the worst public high school in the city and forcing his way into Bishop Gorman, even though she was only a chambermaid in one of the downtown *grind joints* and couldn't afford the tuition. She wouldn't even accept the money the pastor of St. Joan of Arc church offered her in the hope of saving her son from a life in the streets—a life the pastor was certain would lead in a straight line to the maximum security prison in Ely. She chose instead to take a second job and work another twenty hours a week. If her son was going to a private school—Catholic or not—he wasn't going there as a charity case. She was convinced that charity was for losers and she was determined to see that her son came out a winner. Over and over again, she had repeated this to her friends and to her shift bosses and to anyone else who would listen. All of this because his mother was hell-bent on proving what a mistake his father had made in deserting them when Gibb was ten years old.

Gibb did not go to Bishop Gorman willingly. He hated the idea of being thrown in with a bunch of rich kids and having to leave his boyhood friends behind so that his mother could prove her point. There was also the matter of homework. Gangbangers in his neighborhood were very suspicious of kids who did homework and Gibb had the bruised knuckles to prove it. Worse yet, he lacked the training and the discipline required of his classmates who were driven to succeed at an academic high school. This was the uniformly held view of those faculty members who during his freshman year sent frequent reminders to his mother about his failing grades. Rather than conceding defeat, his mother harassed the Viatorian Brothers into teaching him how to study—which they did for the love of God—and he ended up with high marks and a basketball scholarship to the University of Portland and his ticket out of *the war zone*. This was his mother's proudest accomplishment and whenever Gibb pictured her saying so to people around her his stomach acids started churning— churning because those words made him feel forever guilty about all the sacrifices she had made for him.

Fortunately for Gibb, he was paired with Tim Perkins. Tim was the one who introduced him to the wider world, raising his sights high above *the war zone's* barren landscape. To Gibb, it was obvious that Tim benefited from being around a star athlete with brains enough to keep him from flunking out of school. Tim possessed neither the motivation, nor an academic record worth bragging about. In fact, the opposite was true. Academically, Tim ranked close to the bottom of their class, the same place he ended up in after spending four years at Exeter Academy. Just as all the kings horses and all the kings men couldn't put Humpty Dumpty back together again—neither could all of the Perkins family money and influence convince the admission officers at Stanford and UC Berkeley to look the other way and allow Tim to slip through their turnstiles. Not until these twin disappointments had receded far enough into the background did Tim's parents conclude that he would benefit the most from attending a small Catholic liberal arts college, preferably one close enough to home to allow them to carefully monitor his progress. Their research led them to the University of Portland. And thanks to a generous gift to the Congregation of the Holy Cross, coupled with an impassioned plea for mercy,

Tim was admitted to the freshman class. These latter two turns of fortune's wheel were what brought Gibb and Tim together in the same dorm room. This was the version of his story that Tim confided to Gibb during their first late night macho beer drinking session.

All during his first year of college and beyond, Gibb had been led to believe his friendship with Tim Perkins was rooted in his basketball prowess and his 3.9 grade point average. It wasn't until the middle of their sophomore year that Tim confessed to Gibb he was a lot more interested in the frequency with which the best looking women on campus tumbled Gibb's way, than he was in Gibb's athletic prowess or his academic accomplishments.

Gibb had rugged good looks, straight white teeth and a head of hair that was thick and sandy colored and curly and, the majority of the time, unruly. Women liked him because he was over six feet tall and well built and—some of them said—because they thought he had an interesting face. On campus, he dressed in jeans and cowboy boots and when asked usually said he was from Elko, Nevada—which everyone in Portland, Oregon knew was cowboy country. More often than not, he was mistaken for a ranch hand. Rarely did he admit he was a streets kid from Vegas who never in his life had been on a horse. Not that it made much of a difference which story he told—he was too busy studying and playing basketball and in the off-season, working part-time as a waiter in an upscale restaurant—to have a meaningful social life.

Things could have been different, had his father cared at all. His father was said to have relocated somewhere in the area of Stockton, California along with a pile of money and a second family. What little Gibb knew about his father after he left home Gibb had heard second hand from a friend of his mother. The latest information was more than five years old. Information of this sort seemed to him more like stories from the yellowed pages of old newspapers and, in his mind, was about as useful. If the truth were known, as far as he was concerned, his father had died a long time ago.

Worry about whether taxis operated on Sunday night in small New England towns brought Gibb back to reality. He hadn't asked Tim for advice on this subject and now he was sorry. Slinging his carryall over his shoulder, he hoisted his duffel bag to his side and marched over to the staircase leading to the parking lot below. The wind was blowing harder now. It cut through his khakis and sent shivers the length of his body, causing him to quicken his pace during his decent.

At the foot of the staircase, he paused and into the darkened parking lot peered anxiously. Off to the left of him, in the shadows of a large elm tree, he saw the outlines of a four-door sedan. It was Art Donovan waiting in the town taxi for the last train to arrive. The taxi was an older vintage without the usual roof light, making it hard for Gibb to spot. Art was smoking a cigarette and staring at Gibb with a blank look.

Gibb approached the front door of the taxi. Through the open window, Art introduced himself as the owner of the Chatham Taxicab Company—the name that was painted in big letters along the doors of the green and white sedan. Cold as the temperature was, it had not discouraged Art from wearing a short-sleeved Hawaiian shirt and summer straw hat. Gibb stared at Art's heavily lined face and ugly thick-framed glasses. He guessed that Art had seen his share of hard times.

"Looking for work?" Art asked in a New England accent thick enough to cut with a knife.

"A ride will do," said Gibb.

Gibb carried his baggage around to the trunk of the car. Art flicked his cigarette past Gibb and cracked open the front door. Following behind Gibb, he took his time unlocking the trunk. Gibb stood shivering in the cold night air. He stared at Art's tattooed arms, thinking of stories Tim Perkins had told him about the surliness of the natives in Exeter, New Hampshire. Art's black gabardine trousers were short enough so that anyone standing near him got an unobstructed view of his white cotton socks and black work shoes. The dim trunk light exposed a worn spare tire and an old Army blanket and a greasy assortment of tools. Art took Gibb's baggage from him. He threw it on top of the mess. Gibb winced but held his tongue. Without speaking another word, Art closed the trunk lid and returned to the driver's seat.

Gibb slid into the back seat. He focused on the Saint Christopher medal pinned above the rear-view mirror, thinking about how much his mother feared riding in a taxi without one. Art stared at Gibb's reflection in the rear-view mirror.

"Where to?"

"Hampton Court."

"If you don't mind my asking—what business are you in?"

"Computer sales."

"You must be the new guy from Vegas."

"News travels fast."

"What'd you do with your gold chains?"

"Left them behind when I moved to Oregon."

"I went to Vegas once," said Art. "On one of those junkets. Stayed at the Stardust Hotel when it was run by the mob."

"How'd you make out?"

"Lost three grand at the crap tables. After I had trouble payin' my marker, a couple of torpedoes showed up at my doorstep, threatenin' to break both my legs."

"That all changed when the corporate types took over."

"Only way you could get me back there is to kidnap me."

Art spit a load of phlegm out the window. While easing the taxi out of the parking lot, he glanced in the rear-view mirror, checking on whether Gibb had fastened his seatbelt. He caught Gibb staring at his Hawaiian shirt.

"Wonderin' about the shirt, are yuh? Wear it in honor of Harry Truman. Only President ever had real balls."

Gibb remained silent. He was too tired to engage in a political discussion. He was hoping Art would understand.

"You're here to take over the Big Byte store. Right?"

"Right," said Gibb, emphatically, again trying to signal Art that the last thing he was interested in was any further conversation. Art ignored Gibb's signal.

"Hope you have better luck than poor old Mike O'Brien. They fired him when the place went under. He left town after that. Rest of the help's still there though, praying they don't get laid off. These days, jobs are hard to get."

"I heard New England was a lot better off than the West Coast."

Art flashed a critical look in the rear-view mirror. Gibb settled back in his seat and stared out the side window at the shadowy fall scenery. Being the talkative type, Art launched into a capsule history of Chatham interspersed with comments about his Korean War experiences and his return afterwards to his blue-collar neighborhood in Bridgeport. He told of serving the VA faithfully for twelve years, and of being rewarded with a reduction-in-force notice and a trip to the unemployment line, volunteering that in Bridgeport this was something akin to a death sentence. Fortunately for him, his cousin died and willed him the Chatham taxicab concession. Otherwise, he assured Gibb, he would still be squatting on the front steps of his three-decker, watching the world go by and eating beans out of a can every night.

Not that Art had anything in common with most of the people in these parts. He had no use for the big shots who worked in the high-rise buildings in New Haven and Stamford and elsewhere in the county and who tended their lawns in the new sections on weekends. He cared even less for the Farrells and the Binghams who owned the town.

Art found it hard to believe an Irish Catholic would team up with an old Yankee fart like Ezra Bingham, especially during the 1930s when Catholics were still being treated like dirt. From what the Regulars at the bar of the hotel told him when he first came to town, Aloysius P. Farrell—AP they called him—made a bundle of money being counsel to the railroad. After that, he met up with old man Bingham—a high Episcopalian, if ever there was one. Old man Bingham owned all the beachfront property and when he went broke during the Crash of '29, he was desperate enough to partner with an Irish Catholic. The two of them proceeded to take over the town, lock, stock and barrel.

"There sons run it now," said Art with a belligerent look Gibb could see reflected in the rear-view mirror, "and when they're through their grand kids'll take over. People around here treat them like royalty. The worst of them bow and scrape and do everything but kiss their rings."

Gibb was only half listening. As a native Nevadan, Art's talk about the most influential families being treated like royalty bemused him. In Vegas, rarely were formalities observed. Vegas was a place where the grocery store clerks and bank tellers and workers in the other kinds of retail establishments were used to calling customers by their first names, be they strangers or not. Even though, in a manner of speaking, the casino bosses also owned the town and—even though, reportedly, the wealthiest of them had as much money as the royals—anyone seriously suggesting they be treated as aristocrats would have been greeted with catcalls. What Gibb had no way of knowing was that the Binghams and the Farrells had more influence over the fiefdom of Chatham than did the casino owners over the body politic in the state of Nevada.

Gibb was exhausted from his early morning cross country plane trip and from fighting his way through the baggage claim area at Kennedy Airport and from the seemingly endless wait in the taxi line outside the terminal and from worrying whether he would arrive at Penn Station in time to make the last Amtrak train stopping in Chatham. They passed the stone Protestant churches anchoring the village green on both ends and entered Main Street with its colonial storefronts lining the sidewalks on either side behind rows of parking meters. There was a coffee shop and a pharmacy, a grocery store and a gift shop, a liquor store and a florist and a jeweler and seven other small businesses, the largest being Bingham's Hardware. All of them were closed. They were lighted only by street lamps.

Art tipped his hat as they passed the Big Byte store.

"Sounds like a company town," was all the response Gibb could muster to Art's capsule history of Chatham.

"You haven't heard the half of it. They brought in the harps and the wops to do all the dirty work and they kept all the profits for themselves. The harps and the wops that stayed are still blue-collar. Those that were lucky enough to get a college education moved away."

The more Art talked, the more Gibb felt like an alien. He was tempted to tell Art about what a company town Vegas was—the only difference being that most of the blue-collar workers wore white shirts—and where being included in the biggest business deals depended on how much *juice* a person had. His mother always said there was more democracy when the mob ran the town. This did not bother Gibb. To one degree or another, he assumed it was the same everywhere. Besides, changing the world never had been one of his priorities.

About a mile north of the town green, in the midst of a heavily wooded stretch of the Boston Post Road, Art turned off at an unmarked intersection. In the darkness, the taxi's headlights scanned a series of knee high stone walls lining both sides of the narrow country road. Open fields lay beyond the walls and behind them a line of tall trees stood out against the moonlit skyline. Half a mile further on, they came upon a wide driveway flanked by gas lamps, leading to clusters of new one-story, one and two bedroom attached housing units. Outside the entrance, on a large wooden sign, the name *Hampton Court* was painted in gold letters.

Art pulled into the nearest parking space and switched off the ignition. He exited ahead of Gibb, hastily moving around to open the trunk. Fare in hand, Gibb followed close behind him.

"You available to drive me to work in the morning?"

Art handed Gibb his card.

"Don't suppose the boys can hold that against me. All I'll need is about twenty minutes lead time."

Gibb nodded in agreement. Art tipped his hat. He got back into his taxi and drove off. Gibb scanned the housing complex, searching for the location of his unit. All of the buildings had grass courtyards with flagstone walkways leading to the entrances. Their Colonial wood facades were painted gray with green shutters. Carriage lamps illuminated the front entrances.

Gibb trudged up the walkway to his unit. He dropped his baggage alongside the front door mat. Following the realtor's instructions, he reached under the mat for the key. The front door opened into a small entrance-way separating the living room from the kitchen. Gibb switched on the overhead light. He was greeted by a sparsely furnished frigid interior. From where he was standing, light green wall-to-wall carpeting reached all the way to a raised stone fireplace at the opposite end of the living room. A vinyl covered sofa and a recliner with matching ottoman were situated on either side of the fireplace facing each other, with a bare maple coffee table between them. Except for a few inexpensive framed prints of ducks and seagulls hanging on the walls, and end tables and their brass lamps bracketing the sofa, there were no other living room furnishings.

Gibb was not offended in the least. He was used to sparsely furnished apartments. This one wasn't any better or worse than the one he had vacated in Seattle on such short notice. Only this time, as an incentive to relocate, corporate headquarters had made the arrangements and guaranteed his one-year lease. That was all the time he'd been given to rescue the Big Byte store.

Chapter

2

The next morning, Art Donovan dropped off Gibb in front of the Big Byte store and wished him luck. Gibb stood on the sidewalk, shielding his eyes with his hands, staring through the plate glass window at the scene inside. Store hours were nine to six, said the sign posted on the front door. Gibb was half an hour early. All around him, leaves were turning glorious shades of yellow and red under a blue and perfectly clear sky. On the advice of his patron—the General Manager of the Big Byte Corporation—he was dressed in the traditional New England style—Ralph Lauren sport coat, khaki pants and a blue button down Oxford shirt adorned by a brightly colored Brooks Brothers tie. From his earliest days at the Big Byte Corporation, his patron had drilled into his head the importance of making a good first impression on the employees.

To Gibb, the interior of the store seemed congested and out of date. The walls were painted a somber dark brown, matching the dark wood counters. On the counters, there were several rows of PCs and laptop computers and notebook computers randomly placed and racks containing software and accessories and video games and computer guidebooks and magazines. He assumed the store's old-fashioned look was at least partially responsible for it having the lowest gross sales per square foot of any Big Byte store in the company's New England territory.

The employees were milling around inside staring back at him. A well-groomed brunette with a pleasant face and a weight problem came forward to unlock the door. She introduced herself as Gerry Morgan—the Training Director and part time salesperson. Gibb judged her to be in her middle thirties. Partial to tweed suits and silk blouses and sensible shoes—she fit perfectly Tim Perkins's description of a typical middle class New Englander.

"In case you haven't heard, we're down to six people, including me," said Gerry.

Fingering her single strand of pearls, she led him to a square-shaped Formica checkout counter positioned at the center of the store. A high school graduate Gerry introduced to Gibb as Janet Purdy stood behind the cash register with her hands on the counter. Janet looked nervous and she acted nervous. Using hand signals, she summoned to her side of the counter two frail-looking young men. The frail-looking young men introduced themselves as the inside sales staff. Their names were John Rigby and Darryl Dalton. John and Darryl were in their mid-twenties. Both wore rimless eyeglasses and argyle short-sleeved sweaters and knit ties with knots too large for their button-down collars. Neither of them gave the slightest hint of being aggressive enough to be successful salesmen. Gibb stared at the two of them, thinking he now had a better understanding of why this store's sales were so pathetic.

Taking Gibb by the arm, Gerry guided him to the back of the store.

"The service rep and the delivery boy are out on calls," said she. "Their names are Dave Thornton and Tom Browne. Dave's our computer software whiz. Most of the time, he's in the field taking care of extended warranty claims. Tom's a high school kid. He works after classes are let out and on weekends and holidays. There you have it."

The back of the store was equally divided between the training room and the file room. The training room was equipped with a whiteboard and three rows of PCs set on long narrow tables and spaced equidistant apart. One half of the file room served as the lunch area. The lunch area was sparsely furnished. In the center there was a picnic table with bench seats and room enough for ten people. At the far end, a counter with a sink in the center and cabinets overhead ran the length of the wall. On the counter there was a coffee maker and an assortment of coffee mugs and a small box filled with spoons and sugar packets and coffee creamers and paper napkins. The refrigerator was positioned against the wall on the left side close to the counter. On the opposite side of the room in the corner nearest the counter's end an open door led to the manager's office.

Gerry poured Gibb a cup of coffee. She handed him the mug. While adding sugar and cream, Gibb asked her for the sales printouts for the first half of the year. She pointed to the row of black metal file cabinets that stretched from one end of the wall opposite the lunch area all the way to the other end. A metal table and four metal chairs occupied the center of that half of the room. Gerry pointed to an open cardboard box sitting in the middle of the table. Gibb handed her his coffee mug. He picked up the box and carried it into the manager's office. Gerry followed close behind.

The manager's office was a cubbyhole barely large enough for a metal desk and a two-drawer metal filing cabinet and for two people to sit down. It lacked any semblance of authority. A round wood-framed Seth Thomas clock was the only wall fixture. Gibb placed the box of printouts on top of the desk. Gerry handed him his cup of coffee and closed the door behind her.

Gibb sat in the chair behind the desk. He buried his face in his hands, wondering whether he had made a serious career mistake in letting his patron talk him into taking over a bankrupt franchise in a town as small as Chatham. Before Gibb had a chance to ask the obvious question, his patron had explained to him that the Big Byte Corporation's primary interest in saving this store was its strategic location within a 15-mile radius of a number of important high volume users of computer equipment. The fact that the local school system bought more computers than many of the surrounding school districts was an additional consideration. So was the fact that the rent was dirt cheap, his patron had said with a smile on his face.

The day of his departure from Seattle, his patron had taken him aside and in the strictest confidence informed Gibb that for the past twelve months despite a lot of prodding the regional headquarters in Boston had failed to capture its share of business in the state of Connecticut. With a proverbial wink and a nod, the GM disclosed to Gibb that, unbeknownst to the Boston Regional Manager, he was also being sent to Chatham to act as a lightening rod.

Culling repeat sales prospects from the printouts was Gibb's next order of business. He pushed away from the desk, hung his jacket on the hook behind the door, unbuttoned his cuffs and rolled up his sleeves. Then he got to work. As the morning progressed, Gerry brought him a second cup of coffee and tried to engage him in conversation. Making a show of trying to concentrate, he shooed her away. She broadcast his business-like demeanor to the other employees, sending them scurrying about the store straightening out the displays and polishing the workstations.

By mid-afternoon, foot traffic had dwindled to the point where the store was empty of customers. Gibb decided to pounce upon the help while they were loitering about exchanging nervous looks. He marched over to the checkout counter—waving over his head the company manual on how to maximize sales opportunities—signaling for the staff to gather around. The four employees stood at attention on the opposite side of the checkout counter from him. All except Gerry looked crestfallen and fearful. The look on Gerry's face was noncommittal.

"This is the sorriest goddamned operation I've ever seen," said Gibb. "Even worse than Portland when I took over." Pausing for effect, he took a deep breath and exhaled loudly. "Listen up! Either you people shape up or you'll be shipping out. Understand?"

All heads nodded, solemnly.

Gibb took a notepad out of his back pocket. Slapping it on the counter, he pointed his index finger at John and Darryl and directed at them a look intended to be intensely intimidating. John and Darryl reacted as though they were worried about being shot.

"Here's a list of customers that should be ripe for add-ons," said Gibb in the command voice. "By next week, I expect to see some heavy traffic—or else! So you two better forget about closing time and start hitting the phones."

Gibb turned and marched back to his office. All eyes were trained on him. He could hear Gerry saying in imitation of him—"*Big Byte bites back!*" His lecture had the desired effect. It kept everyone working until an hour past closing time. To Gibb's satisfaction, the power of the paycheck had reasserted itself.

At seven o'clock, Gerry walked into Gibb's office over her shoulder carrying the jacket of her tweed suit.

"You do have a way with women," said she, draping her jacket over the back of the extra chair beside Gibb's desk.

Gibb flashed an irritated look at her.

"What are you talking about?"

Gerry began gesturing dramatically with her hands, drawing out her words.

"Janet's in the training room with John and Darryl raving about your sandy hair and your rugged good looks and your sexy hazel eyes and your tall beautiful body—"

Gibb's face turned crimson. He jumped up from his desk.

"Cut it out!"

"I thought you'd be interested in knowing rumors are flying that a Vegas hustler's in town to take over the store." Gibb looked askance. "Not to worry—I told the gossip mill you didn't look like a Vegas hustler."

"What would you know about Vegas hustlers?"

"Only what I learned after Regional told me you were coming and I downloaded that *De Niro* movie *Casino* from Netflix."

Gerry picked Gibb's sports jacket off the hook behind the door and examined it closely.

"One thing's for sure. None of the characters in *Casino* ever heard of Ralph Lauren. Not that your clothes are likely to change any minds around here."

"Get this straight! I'm not here to make friends. I'm here to make sales and—*if sales don't pick up in a hurry*—all of you are history."

Gerry was not intimidated. She responded calmly.

"Is it true what Regional said about you—that you rescued a bigger store in Portland and set sales records in Seattle for three years running?"

"That's yesterday's news."

"I take it you have a plan."

"For starters, we can try bringing this store into the 21st Century."

"What do you have in mind?"

"Ever been in an Apple Store?"

"Once, in New York City."

"That's the look we're imitating on the West Coast. Starting with the shiny grey walls and digital wall displays."

"How are we supposed to afford that?"

"It's in the budget."

"What budget."

"The one Corporate promised me to get me to come here."

"That would be a switch. Regional wouldn't give Mike O'Brien any support whatsoever. The Regional Manager thought Mike was an uncouth Irishman who wasn't right for Big Byte's image. I wonder how George Collingswood III will react having to deal with a store manager from Las Vegas?"

"If he doesn't like it, he can take it up with Corporate. Don't tell George the Third, but I'll be reporting directly to the GM."

Gerry handed Gibb his jacket.

"Can I interest you in a drink?" she asked.

"You bet."

✿ ✿ ✿

Gerry owned a red Nissan sports car and she drove it very fast. In a matter of minutes they were entering the parking lot of the Chatham Beach Hotel.

"This is where the natives hang out," said Gerry. "Except during the tourist season."

The Chatham Beach Hotel was a wooden relic situated on a stretch of beach overlooking Long Island Sound. Its unpainted shingles had a weathered look common in that part of the country. The trim was painted white. According to what Gerry informed Gibb, the hotel was built in the 1920s when money was plentiful. A few sand dunes and a small sandy beach was all that separated the hotel from the water. On the oceanside, the dining area opened onto a wide deck. The deck merged into a porch extending the entire length of the back of the hotel. Gibb remembered seeing pictures of buildings like this in a coffee table book at Tim Perkins's house in Seattle.

Gerry parked her car near the stone jetty separating the hotel property from the town beach and led Gibb back across an unmarked expanse of asphalt parking lot to the side entrance. A short flight of stairs led to a high-ceilinged room decorated in a nautical theme. Overhead, thick cross beams anchored the roof. A series of bay windows looked past the deck to the ocean. In the center of the room there was a four-sided bar, encircled above by stem glasses hanging from wooden racks. The bar was made of mahogany, its center area stacked with the usual assortment of liquor bottles. Outside of a wide oak hardwood apron, wooden tables and captain's chairs were arranged in rows, and along the far wall opposite the side of the bar situated the farthest away from the dining area there were large wooden pegs for hanging coats and foul weather gear. A sound system operated by the bartender played hit tunes from the past at low volume.

The bar stools on the side opposite the dining area—closest to where the coats and foul weather gear hung—were occupied by a post-season assortment of middle-aged townies. All of them were wearing work clothes, their baseball caps resting squarely on their heads. Art Donovan was the exception. Despite the chilly weather, he was still wearing his short-sleeved Hawaiian shirt and his summer straw hat.

Gibb and Gerry walked past the bar. Gerry nodded at Mark Hogan. The white- haired Irishman was standing behind the bar with his arms crossed. Gibb thought he looked like an old fashioned Western saloonkeeper. Gerry whispered to Gibb that Mark had been the hotel bartender for as long as any of the townies could remember.

Art was accorded the end stool on the basis of seniority and most of the time he talked down about Chatham. This was according to Gerry. It was said that his townie friends put up with his insults because Art was a combat veteran and, to the man, they were very patriotic. Not, however, patriotic enough to hang out at the VFW hall, because it was a crummy place and it didn't serve food any longer. Most of their time, they spent drinking draught beer and swapping stories about the Vietnam War and in deference to Art, on occasion, the Korean War.

The townies in loud voices were trading rumors about the *Vegas hustler* they heard was in town to take over the Big Byte store. When Art saw Gerry and Gibb, he motioned to the townies to quiet down and in a lowered voice told them to watch what they were saying about the new Big Byte manager. Abruptly, the townies fell silent. In a resentful manner, they stared down at their beer mugs.

Gerry took Gibb by the arm. She guided him towards a table beside the center bay window. Art folded his arms, glancing at Gibb out of the corner of his eye. With his partially concealed right hand, he waved at Gibb surreptitiously.

"Who are those guys?" Gibb asked, pointing over his shoulder at the townies.

"The usual suspects," said Gerry. "The garage owner, his chief mechanic, the town landscape architect, the head of Environmental Services, the manager of Bingham's Hardware. We call them the *Regulars.*"

"Reminds me of the characters who hang around small town bars in Washington State."

"They're very provincial and very suspicious of strangers, if that's what you mean."

"Like I said before—I'm not here to make friends—I'm here to make sales."

"It's hard to believe someone who dresses like you is from a place like Las Vegas."

"I cleaned up my act when I made it to the U. of Portland."

"The Holy Cross fathers. Right?"

"Right."

"Does that make you a Catholic?"

"I was born and raised one—if that's what you're asking."

"I'd be happy to drive you to Mass on Sundays. It's a great place to meet people."

"I'm afraid God and I are not on speaking terms."

"How long has this been going on?"

"Since I found out God doesn't give a damn about people who live in trailer parks."

"You don't look like the trailer park type."

"That was a long time ago in another galaxy."

A tall, shapely cocktail waitress interrupted them, asking for their drink orders. For as long as he dared, Gibb inspected the cocktail waitress from head to foot. What he saw, he liked. Dark brown hair framed a face highlighted by green eye shadow. She was blessed with straight white teeth and a smooth complexion. Her skintight jeans and her T-shirt emblazoned with a rock band emblem gave her the earthy uninhibited looks of a person who was as desirable as any girl he had seen in a long time. He judged her to be in her late twenties and—although unpolished—good looking enough for him to classify her as a real hottie. Whose hottie, he intended to find out from Gerry.

Gerry ordered a White Russian.

"An old fashioned drink," said Gibb.

"In case you haven't noticed, everything in this town is old fashioned," said the cocktail waitress with one hand on her hip and the other aiming her order pad at Gibb.

"Draft beer for me," said Gibb, wondering about the cocktail waitress's nationality.

The cocktail waitress turned and moved back towards the bar, swinging her hips provocatively.

"Her name is Sally Kilgore," said Gerry. "She's half Irish and half Lebanese and—before you ask—she belongs to Mel Price, the muscle bound creep who runs the local health club. Mel specializes in aerobics classes for bored housewives. Sally's too much of a good time girl to figure out what's going on. Anyway, that's what people around here think."

"I take it you're a native."

"Third generation."

"Then you understand how this town works?"

Gerry nodded affirmatively.

"What's the reason sales are so bad?"

"These days, we're a bedroom community. Most people commute to jobs in the county. During the week they're not around long enough for John and Darryl to get a shot at them."

"Anyone thought about staying open at night?"

"In the off-season, this town closes up early."

"I'm surprised Regional isn't all over you."

"It's obvious, you don't know much about George Collingswood III. That little Harvard twit pays us about as much attention as he does to the monkeys in the Bronx Zoo. We haven't had a visit from him in over three years."

Sally brought their drinks. She dropped two coasters on the table and set the drinks down on top of them.

"Is it always this quiet around here?" Gibb asked Sally.

"My significant other doesn't allow me to talk to strangers," said Sally, again moving away swinging her hips.

"A little rusty are we?" Gerry asked Gibb.

Gibb blushed.

"Where do people go for a good time?"

"The ones with money hang around the Yacht Club. The peasants come here."

"That's it?"

"Unless you're up to driving to New Haven at night. And that would be hard to do without a car."

"Looks like I'll have to try and hit on Sally."

"If you do, Mel and his biker friends are liable to run you over with their Harleys."

The side door opened and shut with a bang, announcing the arrival of a potbellied man in a blue police uniform. Art Donovan and the other Regulars waved to Caleb Nickerson. Caleb Nickerson was the chief of the town's six-man police force. Sally poured a cup of coffee. She set it down for him on the end of the bar. He placed his service cap on the bar alongside his coffee cup and passed the time of day with Sally. Gerry warned Gibb that Caleb was as distrustful of strangers as any of the Regulars and very protective of Sally. She told him that Sally was dating Mel Price against Caleb's advice and that Caleb talked openly of his determination to arrest Mel and force him to leave town. It was rumored that Mel was equally as determined to deny Caleb the excuse he sought, knowing as he did that in Caleb's mind something as inconsequential as more than one parking ticket might be sufficient to unleash upon Mel the dogs of war.

The Regulars drank up and left early. Gerry said they were afraid if they lingered too long their wives would call and raise hell with Mark Hogan. Mark had been the hotel bartender for thirty years and had attended every one of their weddings. It comforted the wives to know where their husbands did their drinking after work. They depended on Mark to alert them if ever trouble arose. Gibb was not surprised at hearing this. He had witnessed this particular tribal custom in action in other neighborhood bars in the West and was thankful he was a bachelor.

Gibb's line of sight was intersected by a black teenager in a white busboy's jacket carrying a plastic tray. He was heading towards a pile of dirty dishes on a nearby table. From Gibb's limited observation of life in Chatham, the busboy stood out like a sore thumb. Pausing before cleaning off the table, the busboy motioned to Gerry.

"Hello, Miss Morgan," he said laboriously, in the manner of a retarded child.

"How's it going, Smitty?"

Smitty was short and chubby and his head was lopsided.

"Everything's cool."

"Say hello to Gibb Quinn. Gibb's my new boss."

"Pleased to meet you, Mister Gibb."

"We'll get along better if you skip the *Mister*."

"Whatever you say Mister Gibb."

Smitty bussed the table and moved away towards the kitchen.

"He's the first black person I've seen in this town," said Gibb.

"That's because there's never been more than a handful of black families living here and they keep a low profile."

"How did he manage to slip in?"

"Saint Joseph's orphanage put the arm on Judge Farrell. He convinced Heather Caldwell to give Smitty a job. Heather owns the hotel."

"Smitty looks retarded."

"He is retarded."

"That must have been tough for the natives to swallow."

"Heather didn't mind. Her grandfather was an African missionary. The rest of the townspeople figured that being retarded he wouldn't cause them any trouble."

"Meaning?"

"Meaning, he's not likely to be asking anyone's daughter for a date."

"Does Chatham have an open housing law—or is he bussed in?"

"He sleeps in a room above the hotel garage."

Chapter

3

By September's end, Gibb realized the odds were against his being able to garner enough business from the town of Chatham and its immediate surroundings to meet the monthly sales goals his patron had set for him. The best opportunities, he knew now, lay elsewhere in places like New Britain and Hartford to the north of Chatham and New Haven and Norwalk and Stamford to the south, where most of the corporate offices were located. He was well aware that a major sales move beyond his assigned territory would antagonize his Regional Manager. Whenever they were faced with situations involving violations of the company manual's first commandment—*Salesmen shall not make sales outside their assigned territory*—uppermost in the minds of Big

Byte's super salesmen was the risk-reward ratio. After enough late-night deliberation, Gibb concluded that the potential rewards outweighed the risks by a wide enough margin to justify taking the gamble.

In order to reach his targets he needed transportation. His patron obliged by authorizing him on a trial basis to lease a rental car in the company's name. The car was all the logistical support he required in order to launch his one-man sales drive in earnest. Anxious to test his salesmanship against what Tim Perkins had warned him was the ingrained skepticism of New Englanders, he sallied forth with one eye fixed on Boston and the other eye fixed on Seattle.

It was not long before he discovered that, in the case of the sales targets he selected, New England skepticism was not a strong enough antidote to counteract the Las Vegas mystique. Most of these Information Technology managers, at one time or another either had been to Las Vegas attending business conventions or were hoping for any excuse to visit *the entertainment capital of the world*—some more openly than others. Those who were fans of Las Vegas were mesmerized by what they had seen or heard about its *Sin City* image. With a wink or a poke in the ribs, or both, they were quick to quote to him the discarded slogan—*What plays in Vegas, stays in Vegas.* Those who when in the presence of other employees claimed not to be fans often took him aside, acknowledging in whispers that, if ever they were tempted to engage in sinful behavior, Las Vegas would be their first choice.

And so it came to pass that, from a salesman's perspective, being labeled a "Vegas guy" turned out to be a large plus for Gibb, instead of the minus Tim Perkins had warned him about. Gibb used this to great advantage by importuning those street-wise friends of his who at major hotels on *the Strip* had risen to the rank of pit boss or doorman or bell captain. From them he was able to extract the complimentary offerings he used to reward his best corporate customers.

This tactic worked well enough for Gibb to set sales records in the months of October and November. He taped to the wall of his office the congratulatory emails from his patron written in capital letters and set his sights even higher. Each congratulatory email was accompanied by an equally demonstrative email complaint from his Regional Manager. The latter ones, he also taped to the wall side by side with the congratulatory ones.

At this point in their relationship, Gibb and George Collingswood III were engaged in a weekly minuet. Collingswood III would place a telephone call to Gibb to berate Gibb for continuing to make sales calls outside of his assigned territory. Each time, Gibb would invite Collingswood III to direct his complaint to the Big Byte General Manager. On the one hand, the General Manager would agree to counsel Gibb to cease violating company policy while, on the other hand, advising Gibb to keep up the good work. And there the matter stood, unresolved and festering.

Saturday evenings during the month of October, Gibb visited the bar at the Chatham Beach Hotel and tried without success to coax Sally Kilgore home with him. Gibb was attracted by her sensual good looks and by the vulnerability he sensed lay beneath the surface and by the empathy he felt for a girl whose background mirrored his and by the conviction that, if given the opportunity, he could help save her from herself. During each visit, he was careful to sit at a window table at the end of the dining area, far enough away to prevent the bar patrons from overhearing their conversations.

Sometimes when the bar was less busy, Sally spoke to him openly about her alcoholic mother and about how her father had deserted them when she was thirteen years old and about her childhood spent in a run-down three-decker in Bridgeport. Gibb learned that before she became overwhelmed by cynicism she had dreams of attending community college and of abandoning the life of a barmaid for a *respectable* daytime job in an office. These were dreams fostered by college men she had dated. Men who pretended to be more interested in her free spirit and her earthy sense of humor than in her body, men who made love to her and left her when the thrill was gone. Having given up on the idea of escaping, she was determined to live only for the moment. This had made her an irresistible target of opportunity for Mel Price.

Sally reminded Gibb of the girl he dated during his junior and senior years at Bishop Gorman. Maria Martinez was an authentic wild one—a good-looking girl with a raw sense of humor and zero inhibitions. She was a senior at Western High, one of the roughest high schools in Vegas. Her mother was an alcoholic, her father a small time drug dealer. After her best friend died of an overdose, Maria switched from smoking crack cocaine to drinking straight shots of Jose Cuervo, chasing them down with Corona Light. On the nights when she was not waiting on tables at a Mexican restaurant, Maria was a member of a Latino drag racing team. When Gibb first met her, driving fast cars and drinking tequila were her favorite pastimes. She told Gibb she was attracted to him because he was a star basketball player on a winning team and also because he was as tough as any of the gangbangers who lived in her neighborhood.

Tears were streaming down Maria's face the day that Gibb read her the letter from the University of Portland announcing his scholarship grant, signifying to her that their romance was coming to an end. Gibb kept in touch during his college years. With his encouragement she became a baccarat dealer at one of the high-end Strip hotels. The amount of money she made as a baccarat dealer allowed her to escape from the barrio to a one-bedroom apartment in a middle class neighborhood and to marry a car salesman at a Lexus dealership. Gibb was as proud of her accomplishments as she was of his.

Convinced by his experience with Maria that getting involved with Sally also could have a happy ending, Gibb pursued her as methodically as he did every IT manager who resisted his sales advances. But hard as he tried, Sally kept him at arms length. From all appearances, figuratively speaking, Sally was wedded to Mel Price.

Gibb was ready to concede defeat when on a rainy November evening his luck changed. It happened towards the end of another very busy week. He had fallen asleep in front of the TV set in his living room. The remains of a TV dinner and a half-empty bottle of beer lay abandoned on the coffee table. He was jolted awake by the persistent, intermittent, irritating sound of the doorbell. Stumbling over to the front door, he rubbed his eyelids with his palms. When he opened the door, Sally Kilgore was leaning against the doorframe dressed in skintight jeans, a denim jacket and aerobic shoes. She was smoking a joint.

Gibb asked her whether she was sure she had the right address? Sally laughed.

"I am now stud."

"Your significant other fall off his bike and land on his head?"

"He's spending the night in New Haven with his hoodlum buddies."

"And?"

"I'm thirsty and I thought you might buy me a drink."

Gibb pointed to the kitchen.

"Help yourself."

Sally unbuttoned her jacket and tossed it towards the living room sofa. Switching off the TV set, Gibb followed her to the kitchen. Sally pulled open the refrigerator door and withdrew an open bottle of white wine and a bottle of beer. She handed the bottle of beer to Gibb. Gibb twisted off the cap. Sally removed a stem glass from a kitchen cabinet and poured herself a glass of wine.

Gibb found himself studying Sally's features. She had inherited more of her looks from the Lebanese side of her family than from the Irish side. Her dark brown eyes gave her a sultry look. They had Gibb thinking that were she from an affluent family she could have had her pick of any man in town, instead of settling for a drug peddling biker.

Sally took a gulp of wine. Retrieving her joint from an ashtray on the kitchen counter, she offered the joint to Gibb. Gibb shook his head from side to side.

"Tell me about Vegas," said Sally.

"Move in with me and I'll take you there for a weekend."

Sally placed her arms around Gibb's neck and kissed him hard.

"Let's just take it one day at a time," said she, pressing her tongue in his ear.

Ten days later was the first time Gibb had been back to the hotel bar since his visit from Sally. The hands of the wall clock were at 10:00 p.m. The bar was deserted. Mark Hogan was seated behind the bar on a stool reading the *New Haven Register*. At the near end of the bar, the Chief of Police rested on his elbows, drinking coffee and chatting with Sally. Gibb walked past them to a seat at a window table. Sally interrupted her conversation with the chief to bring Gibb a mug of draft beer.

"Is it too late to order a hamburger?"

"Not if you promise to eat fast. Mark says we're closing early. This place has been dead tonight."

"I promise, I'll be quick."

Sally leaned over the table and whispered in Gibb's ear.

"After the chief leaves, I'll follow you home."

Gibb was halfway through his meal when the chief put on his service cap and waved goodbye to Mark Hogan. Gibb finished his hamburger. He left ahead of Sally. Theirs were the only two cars in the parking lot. Gibb placed his key in the door lock. Sally came up behind him. She punched him lightly on the shoulder. He turned around.

"How come you didn't call me?"

"I figured you were just getting even with Mel for something."

"You got that right."

"What will Mel say if you don't make it home tonight?"

"Fuck Mel!"

"I take it you already have."

"And then some," Sally said sarcastically.

"The chief wouldn't like you talking like this."

"No more than he'd like it, if he knew I was planning to shack up with a stud from Vegas. Chief's no different than the townies that hang around the bar after work. They all figure your're hiding something or hiding from something. Either way, don't expect to win any popularity contests."

✿ ✿ ✿

A week later, Sally moved her belongings into Gibb's apartment. After that life was satisfying and so was Sally and Gibb was content. His contentment lasted until the December day a week before Christmas when Alicia Farrell and her mother walked into the Big Byte store during a 12" snowstorm. Alicia had classic blonde looks from out of the pages of a fashion magazine. She was smartly dressed in a full-length wool coat, tan wool pants, a navy blue turtleneck sweater, and leather boots. Her mother, a handsome, well groomed woman in her late forties, paused to brush the snow from her full-length mink coat. Darryl approached them, asking if he could be of assistance. Alicia told Darryl that she and her mother were interested in purchasing a personal computer.

Gibb was standing near the cash register talking to Gerry and Janet, staring at Alicia. When Alicia's boarding school accent bounced off his libido, he was tempted to ask for her hand in marriage. Gerry waved at Alicia. Alicia waved back at her. Leaning over next to him, she whispered to Gibb.

"That's Alicia Farrell and her mother. You'd better start sucking up to them."

This being Gibb's first ever encounter with a Farrell or a Bingham, it brought to mind Art's carrying on about the two families being looked upon as royalty. Gibb decided that closing a sale with a member of a royal family had a lot better chance of succeeding than a marriage proposal. Exhaling noticeably, he stepped forward and eased Darryl aside.

"This is Mr. Quinn, our manager," said Darryl.

"I heard you say you were interested in a personal computer," said Gibb to Alicia, smiling his best salesman's smile. "PCs come in all shapes and sizes. Tell me what you're planning to use it for and I can suggest some alternatives."

"It's not for us," said Alicia. "It's a Christmas present for my father—Judge Farrell."

"Most likely my husband will use it for writing opinions at home, and for communicating online with the clerk's office," said Mrs. Farrell. "What make do you recommend?"

"Would the judge prefer a desktop or a laptop?"

"If the truth were known, he would prefer not to have one, at all," said Alicia. "We've decided a desktop would be best for him."

"You can save money by buying one of our Big Byte models. Otherwise, I'd recommend an HP. Hewlett-Packard is a technology powerhouse—besides, it's one of the companies that's been around the longest."

"Aside from the laptop my parents bought for me when I was in college and the Dell at my uncle's law office, I don't know one brand from another," said Alicia.

"I'm very much in favor of old established companies," said Alicia's mother.

Alicia laughed.

"And old established everything else," said she.

"Old companies are like old families," said Mrs. Farrell. "They have tradition to uphold. That makes them more dependable. If we decide to buy one, we'll want the very best."

Gibb had been studying the two of them, trying to decide which sales approach would allow him to close the sale at the highest price. Alicia's mother seemed to him to personify all the virtues of this old New England town—she was cheerful and earnest and very polite. He imagined that she would have gotten along well with the Perkins family.

"I'd recommend a high-end HP with the Windows 7 operating system and lots of memory—and, a printer, of course."

"If we take your recommendation, will you promise to bring it out and set it up for us?" Alicia's mother asked.

"I'll even throw in free lessons."

"Sold to the lady in the mink coat," said Alicia's mother, offering Gibb her gloved hand. "Send us an estimate, as soon as you can. We'll need to have it delivered and installed the day before Christmas."

Gibb walked with Alicia and her mother to the front door. He watched them pick their way through the snow to a Lincoln sedan parked at the curb, thinking that Alicia was the most beautiful girl he had ever seen. When he turned back around, he found himself face to face with Gerry.

"If you can keep the former Elisabeth Davenport happy, she'll send lots of customers our way. She's a Boston Brahmin—one of the Mayflower crowd."

"As in moving vans?"

"As in small boats."

"Actually—I'm more interested in her daughter."

"Unfortunately for you, the Belle of Chatham Township is already spoken for."

"What does she do?"

"She's taking a year off before starting Yale Law School. She's spending it working in her uncle's law office. Tom Farrell represents the family's interests at Bingham and Farrell Properties and on the board of the Chatham Trust Company."

"Tell me about her love life."

"Josh Bingham Jr.'s his name. He was captain of the crew team at Yale. He's in his second year of law school there. They've been dating for ages."

"Doesn't sound like there's much hope for someone like me."

"Not when it's the University of Portland against an all Yale lineup."

"Meaning?"

"Her grandfather—his grandfather—her father—his father—her—him twice. Need I say more?"

"Are they all that smart?"

"Alicia and Josh Jr. are—they both graduated with honors. Some of the others, I'm not so sure. At Yale they're called *legacies.* Anyway, when you're that rich, who says you have to be smart?"

✿ ✿ ✿

The visit of Alicia and her mother to the Big Byte store marked the beginning of the Christmas rush. Gibb was determined to break another sales record in the month of December. He began a series of six-teen-hour workdays interrupted only by sleep and his morning run. Everywhere in the township, the signs of Christmas were on display. Almost without exception, houses and shrubbery were adorned with Christmas lights and the streets were filled with Christmas greet-ings. On the town green a large crèche that no one dared challenge was on display beside the bandstand. It was a winter of record snow storms. And once school was out, snowballs filled the air and sleds every hillside in town.

Gibb placed an advertisement in the local tabloid newspaper delivered free of charge to all of the Chatham residences, offering to match any computer price offered online. Thereafter, the daily crush of cus-tomers at the Big Byte buying desktops and laptops and notebook computers and tablet computers and software of every kind resembled the scene at a New York department store on the day the annual sale was underway. Nothing put Gibb in a better mood than being assured of another record sales month. He moved around the store greeting customers, whispering words of encouragement to Darryl and John, and doing his best to empty the shelves of merchandise. The closer it came to Christmas, the more Gibb thought about Alicia Farrell, hoping she would be at home when he delivered her father's Christmas present.

The afternoon before Christmas, Gibb helped Tom the delivery boy load Judge Farrell's desktop and printer into the company van. The van was parked in the alley behind the store. Gibb was wearing his fleece-lined suede jacket—the type seen in advertisements featuring cowboys smoking filtered cigarettes—and a woolen navy watch cap. Gerry followed them out to the van, lecturing them on the importance of this installation to Big Byte's business prospects.

The delivery boy guided the company van down the back alley to the opening onto Main Street. They circled around the town green past the Methodist Church and the Chatham Trust Company and drove to the most expensive section of town where the houses were big enough and stately enough to qualify as mansions. Each of them was set back a good distance from the road on five acre lots. The lots were surrounded by shrubbery and by tall oak trees and an occasional stand of white birch. Manicured lawns the size of golf fairways were covered by a foot of new snow. Only the roofs of the mansions and their driveways and front walks were cleared, the driveways and front walks right to the edges, as if tended by perfectionists.

By now, Gibb was aware that Chatham was divided along architectural lines. The important families owned either brick colonials in the old sections or Victorian houses situated along the shoreline. Those located along the shoreline shared the beaches with wealthy New Yorkers, mostly. These two groups divided up the memberships at the Chatham Yacht Club and mixed uneasily in the summertime. The latter information, Gibb had gleaned from conversations with Art Donovan, who had heard it from the Regulars and from drunken New Yorkers that on occasion he had ferried from the Yacht Club to their residences.

Gibb did not doubt that the Farrells were very rich. They occupied one of the largest of the white brick colonials with dark green shutters and a front door that matched, situated in the oldest inland section of the town. The delivery boy parked the van in the driveway alongside a flagstone walkway leading to the front door. Gibb got out and made his way to the front door where a Christmas wreath hung from a brass knocker. Through the living room windows he could see a ceiling-high Christmas tree. The tree was ornately decorated.

A maid in a white and black uniform answered the bell. She motioned for Gibb to move around to the garage entrance. Gibb and the delivery boy entered the house through the three-car garage, transporting their cargo on a dolly. The garage was spotless. It was occupied by the Lincoln Alicia and her mother had arrived in the day they visited the Big Byte store, and by a white BMW convertible and a black Mercedes sedan. Gibb guessed that the BMW belonged to Alicia.

The two of them stacked the HP-branded cartons one on top of the other in the hallway leading from the garage to the kitchen. A second uniformed maid opened the kitchen door, cautioning them to be sure and leave their boots behind. When satisfied that they had complied, the second uniformed maid led them single file in their stocking feet through a huge kitchen and out into a carpeted hallway. Gibb was thinking about how embarrassed he would have been, had he holes in his socks.

The computer—the second uniformed maid lectured them in the main hallway—was to be installed in the judge's den. Overcome by a powerful mixture of holly and bayberry candles and pine wreaths, Gibb stopped short. The second uniformed maid gestured towards the back of the house. After pinpointing for him the location of the den, she departed abruptly, leaving Gibb alone with the delivery boy. The sound of Christmas carols coming from another part of the house made Gibb wish he had a family to return home to at Christmastime. It was the time of the year when he missed his mother the most and when he felt the loneliest.

The den was easy to locate. Like all else he had seen of the Farrell mansion, it was richly appointed, featuring leather furniture and a large mahogany desk and a Persian rug woven in a field of maroon and navy blue on an ivory background. Built-in bookcases painted white and lined with law books straddled a large fieldstone fireplace. The fireplace was framed by a carved wooden mantel. Hanging above the fireplace mantel was an oil painting of someone serious from another era. Alicia's paternal grandfather, Gibb speculated, judging by the man's attire. Between the ornate picture frame and the mantel a double-edged sword was mounted.

After the cartons were unpacked, Gibb dispatched the delivery boy back to the store. He was halfway through the work of installing the PC and the printer, when Alicia and Josh Bingham Jr. appeared. Both were dressed casually in corduroy slacks and Yale sweatshirts. They sat down on the Persian rug and leaned against the leather sofa, watching Gibb work and asking enough questions to delay the finish for another hour.

Alicia waited until the PC and the printer were installed and in working order, before leaving to find her mother. Gibb sat on the floor with his back against the desk, waiting for Alicia's mother to appear. Josh Jr. sat cross-legged, facing Gibb. Over six feet tall and lanky, he spoke with the same boarding school accent Tim Perkins had acquired at Exeter.

"I understand you're from Las Vegas," said Josh Jr.

"My last stop was Seattle—I grew up in Vegas."

"Do people actually live there?"

"They tried bussing them in," Gibb said facetiously. "But it didn't work out."

Gibb struggled to conceal his irritation. He had never been able to understand why the mere mention of his hometown caused so many strangers to react negatively, especially people from the East Coast. There were—he was certain—just as many good people in Vegas as there were anywhere else he had ever been. Yet trying to convince the outside world of this was such a losing proposition. He blamed it on the talk shows and the movies, the way the gangster image persisted no matter how hard the Chamber of Commerce tried to erase it. And he wanted to strangle whoever was responsible for promoting the establishment of a museum dedicated to the mobsters that put Las Vegas on the map. This he could never acknowledge to Josh Jr.— Josh Jr. was just too damn superior. He was tempted to say that the Vegas area population was 4.6 times larger than the cities of Bridgeport, New Haven and Hartford combined. But for someone who was about to graduate with honors from one of the top-ranked law schools in the country, Josh Jr. exhibited so little concern for facts, Gibb assumed he would be wasting his time.

He was relieved when Alicia reappeared with her mother.

"Alicia tells me you have it up and running," said the former Elizabeth Davenport.

"All that's left is for you to call us when the judge is ready for his free Windows 7 lessons."

Alicia's mother went to a writing table inlaid with leather. She withdrew a checkbook from a narrow drawer. Leaning over the writing table, she wrote out a check and handed it to Gibb.

"We appreciate your coming out on Christmas eve."

"We're happy to be of service," said Gibb, flashing his best salesman's smile.

"Josh will show you to your car."

"I don't have a car."

"Then Josh will drive you home. Where do you live?"

"Across town—at a place called Hampton Court. But I'd rather walk."

"I don't believe I've ever heard of Hampton Court," said the former Elizabeth Davenport with a quizzical look.

"It's one of the new developments."

"I should have known."

Gibb retrieved his boots from the kitchen hallway. He carried them to the front foyer. Alicia held his cap and coat while he pulled his boots on and tightened the laces. Josh Jr. stood to one side, watching.

"Father will be pleasantly surprised," said Alicia, handing Gibb his cap and coat.

On the walk home, Gibb could not put out of his mind the picture of Alicia and Josh Jr. holding hands in the doorway, wishing him a very Merry Christmas.

✿ ✿ ✿

Gibb was in the kitchen in mid-afternoon on Christmas day when Sally returned from Bridgeport. A stuffed turkey was roasting in the oven. As a surprise, Gibb had bought Sally a bottle of Mount Nelson sauvignon blanc. He was busy packing ice around it in a silver ice bucket he had found in the back of one of the kitchen cupboards. Earlier he had stacked the fireplace andirons with birch logs and kindling wood. The kindling was lighted and the logs were crackling. It was Gibb's way of relieving the plainness of the living room furnishings.

Sally looked terminally unhappy. Without a word of greeting, she dropped her overnight bag on the living room couch and ran to the bathroom. Gibb heard the bathroom door slam shut behind her. He began skinning carrots and cucumbers, hoping that whatever was troubling Sally would not spoil their Christmas dinner.

Half an hour later she reappeared. Her hair wet and without makeup, she marched over to the kitchen cupboard and took down a stem glass. From the refrigerator, she withdrew an open bottle of white wine. Gibb waited while she poured herself a glassful. Moving close to her, he kissed her on the lips.

"Merry Christmas," said he, cheerfully.

Sally burst into tears.

"Problems in Bridgeport?"

"She does it to me every goddamn time. I always swear I'll never go back—and like a little sucker, every year I do."

Gibb wiped her eyes with a paper napkin.

"Want to tell me what happened?"

Sally leaned her back against the kitchen counter and drank half of the wine in her glass. She began speaking rapidly. Her voice was filled with anger. Tears were streaming down both cheeks.

"She was drunk, as usual, and the place looked like a shithouse. It took me until midnight to straighten it out. By that time, she was passed out on the living room couch. I threw out all the booze bottles I could find—like she figured I would. But it didn't do any good. When I woke up this morning, she was half gone again and refusing to eat or go to church. I decided to sit with her till noon. Turned out to be a complete waste of time. After a while, I gave up and told her I had to get back to work. Before I left, I gave her the dress I'd bought for her and wished her a Merry Christmas, hoping she'd be happy for once. Instead, she pulls a half pint out of her bathrobe pocket and says in a loud voice—'*Merry Christmas, you fucking tramp!*' How's that for a Christmas greeting?"

"She was probably depressed about your father walking out on her."

"Shit, Gibb! I can't seem to make you understand my father was a bum—the biggest fucking Irish bum in Bridgeport. He was so bad; he even tried to get into my pants when I was thirteen. And he probably would have, if he hadn't run off to Schenectady with that waitress."

"Maybe your being a cocktail waitress is what's bugging your mother."

"Since when is Mr. Cool a psychiatrist? You're so wrapped up in your fucking computers, you don't know the first thing about real life."

"The hell I don't. I was raised in a trailer park—remember?"

"Trailer park, my ass! You made that shit up because you figured it'd make it easier to get into my pants. You've got better preppie clothes than any of those Yalie faggots that hang around the hotel bar in the summertime?"

"The clothes came after I left Vegas."

"As far as people in Chatham are concerned, you're still from Vegas—and you always will be."

"I don't give a rat's ass where they think I'm from— as long as they buy my computers."

Sally reached into the pocket of her jeans and removed a small leather pouch. She pulled the strings apart, poured a small amount of pot on to a piece of filter paper, and rolled herself a joint. After lighting up, she sat on the edge of the fireplace, sipping wine and dragging on the joint, watching Gibb set the dining room table. It was not long before her tears subsided. Leaning backwards, she took a long drag on her joint, holding the smoke in, and then slowly letting it out.

"On days like this, I wish I was back with Mel," she said, wistfully.

"Mel doesn't have the brains Smitty has."

"Mel thinks Smitty is queer."

"What do you mean by queer? The kid's retarded."

"What makes you think retards can't be queer?"

"Gerry says, sexually he's at the level of a six year old. That's how come they let him work at the hotel in the first place."

"Mel still thinks he's queer."

"Mel's sick."

"At least he keeps a supply of crack around."

"That's because he's a dealer."

"Says who?"

"Art Donovan."

"Art Donovan doesn't know his ass from first base."

Lately, whenever Gibb and Sally talked about Mel Price, Art Donovan wound up in the middle. During the early days, while Art was chauffeuring Gibb to the Big Byte store, Art became Gibb's authority on Mel. This really irritated Sally. Sally did not understand how anyone from Bridgeport could be an authority on any subject. Unless, of course, the discussion was about poverty. Nor did she agree that Mel was a dealer. She was of the opinion that real drug dealers sold to anyone they could, whereas Mel had assured her that he limited his sales activities to a select group of corporate wives who attended his aerobics classes. Mel was referring to those health club members he also provided stud services to when their husbands were out of town. These were the protectors that kept him from being busted by the Chief of Police. Until Gibb offered her a way out, Sally had been willing to overlook Mel's cheating because she depended upon him to supply her with pot. She had confessed all of this to Gibb late one evening when she was stoned. Gibb assumed it was her way of absolving herself of guilt for having allowed Mel to take advantage of her in the first place.

Sally said she was tired of talking about Art and Mel. She broke off the conversation. In her bare feet, she went to the kitchen to inspect the turkey. She yanked open the oven door. The turkey was golden brown and moist. From the smile on her face, Gibb could tell she was impressed.

"Where did a tough guy like you learn to cook a turkey?" she asked.

"Working nights in the catering department of one of the hotels in *Glitter Gulch*."

Again Sally burst into tears.

"God, do I hate Christmas," she said, pounding a fist on a kitchen cabinet.

"Everyone gets lonely, sometimes."

"You never do."

"The hell I don't."

Sally looked at Gibb accusingly.

"I'll bet you'd rather be at the Farrell's—wouldn't you?"

"You're selling yourself short."

"Bullshit, short! My mother's right. I'm nothing but a tramp."

"You ever take Mel to meet her?"

"We once rode down to Bridgeport on his Hog."

"Wearing leather jackets and motorcycle boots, no doubt."

"How'd you guess?"

"No wonder she thinks you're a tramp."

"You still haven't said whether you'd rather be at the Farrell's."

"Wouldn't everyone?"

"You'd better not get any crazy ideas about hitting on Alicia Farrell or believe me the Farrells and the Binghams will make dog meat out of your ass."

Chapter

4

At 8:30 a.m. on the second of January, Gibb was obliged to take a telephone call from George Collingswood III. To say that Collingswood III was highly agitated would have been an understatement. He began the conversation by announcing how anxious he was to share with Gibb his New Year's resolution. *"Cease making sales calls outside your assigned territory or risk being fired!"*—was the message he conveyed to Gibb in a loud angry voice. From the vitriol that followed, Gibb became convinced that Collingswood III regarded insubordination and insurrection as being interchangeable. In defending himself, he made the mistake of telling Collingswood III he did not think making sales outside of his territory rose to the level of the Boston Tea Party. This was more than the Regional Manager could bear. He slammed down the receiver, cutting Gibb off in mid-sentence.

Gibb was unmoved by Collingswood III's threat. It was well known within the Big Byte sales organization that in his salesman days the company's founder had been fired by one of the leading PC manufacturers for the same type of disorderly conduct. The firing had motivated their rebel commander to establish the Big Byte Corporation and—on the day it became a public company—made him into a millionaire many times over. He attributed his success to having enough salesmen patterned after him to overcome the odds on beating the competition. This mantra caused him to turn a deaf ear to the pleas of managers like Collingswood III— all the while insisting for the record that the company manual must be followed to the letter. No wonder the General Manager was willing to overlook Gibb's continuing violations of company policy.

Gibb chose to ignore the fact that the founder was aging and said to be in declining health. It was no secret that Collingswood III was aware of the founder's condition. Their Regional Manager was known to feel it was only a matter of time before Big Byte's technocrats seized control from those swashbuckling senior executives like Gibb's patron who fancied themselves entrepreneurs and who chose repeatedly and brazenly to ignore company protocol. The swashbucklers were known to be guided by the founder's concluding admonition at a sales meeting long ago—"*I want my salesmen out there seven days a week—kicking ass and taking names!*" That same kick-ass attitude is what motivated the General

Manager to enlist Gibb in his stealth program to goose the company's Connecticut sales. In the meantime, Collingswood III and his allies, to the man dedicated to bringing order out of what they regarded as chaos, lay in wait on the sidelines like alligators in a swamp, looking forward to the day when the founder retired.

Lately, in order to ease tensions within the warring camps and to protect himself in case of a sudden change of command, Gibb's patron had advised Gibb to begin treating Collingswood III with the respect to which every Regional Manager was entitled. Gibb knew better than to ignore his patron's advice. Despite his reservations, he resolved to call Collingswood III back and attempt to placate him.

"What is it Quinn?" Collingswood III asked when the receptionist relayed to him Gibb's call.

"I may have found a solution to our problem, George," said Gibb cheerfully.

"Correction, Quinn. You're problem!"

"Whatever."

"I'm waiting."

"I've sold a high-end HP to one of Chatham's biggest hitters. And I'm expecting tons of referrals, which should keep me closer to home base."

Gerry Morgan popped into Gibb's office and leaned over his desk. Silently moving his lips, Gibb informed her that George the Third was on the line. Gerry replied with a pained expression. Thrusting a middle finger at the receiver, she slumped into the chair beside Gibb's desk.

"One other thing, Quinn. At Regional, I'm used to being addressed as Mr. Collingswood."

"I don't recall any mention of that in the manual, George."

"Some things were not meant to be in the manual."

Collingswood III slammed down the receiver loud enough for Gerry to hear.

"Better watch your butt, Gibb."

"You're not here to warn me about George the Third."

"You're right. I came to tell you I ran into Alicia Farrell after Sunday Mass."

Gerry paused for effect.

"And?"

"She asked enough questions about you to convince me she's interested."

"What did you tell her?"

"That you went to Bishop Gorman High and to the University of Portland—that you graduated *magna*—that last year you were admitted to Stanford Business School—but you turned Stanford down because you couldn't face being a pauper again. I also mentioned the *hundred K* in student loans you figured you'd be saddled with. She wasn't pleased when I told her I thought thirty-two was a little old for her."

Gibb's face turned red with embarrassment.

"Why would someone who's engaged be interested in hearing this stuff?"

"Haven't a clue. As far as anyone in this town knows, she's planning to marry Josh Bingham and live happily ever after."

"While she was at it—did she say anything about being engaged?"

"Like Yogi Berra said—'*It ain't over till its over!*'"

✿ ✿ ✿

One week later, Gibb was standing in front of the cash register waiting for Janet to ring up a software sale when Gerry hooked his arm and turned him around towards her.

"How did it go last night?"

"I thought I looked great in my Ralph Lauren blazer and white button down. I even wore my hottest Ferragamo tie—but the judge wasn't fooled for one minute."

"Let me guess. He gave you his—*I don't mind taking computer lessons from you but don't get any ideas about dating my daughter!*—look."

"You know him well."

"I'll bet Alicia was there."

"Right, again. She hinted she'd be more useful to her uncle if she knew more about Windows 7."

"Did you get invited back?"

"For as many lessons as it takes to familiarize the judge with Windows 7."

"By the time he masters that program, you should be a member of the family."

"Not without a Yale degree."

"Maybe you should apply."

"I'll settle for enough referrals to keep George the Third off my back."

Gerry was sitting in Gibb's office when Alicia called to inform Gibb her father was too impatient to try and master Windows 7 and that he wanted her to take advantage of the remaining free lessons. Alicia asked whether sometime that day would be a convenient time for her to visit? Gibb said he would gladly rearrange his schedule to accommodate her. Alicia was so pleased, she offered to supply their lunches.

"Make mine a ham and Swiss on rye," said Gibb, before hanging up.

Gibb turned to Gerry with a grin on his face.

"That was Alicia Farrell."

"So I gathered."

"Her father told her she could have the rest of the free lessons."

"I'll bet it was her idea."

"What makes you think so?"

"She was asking about you again after Mass last Sunday."

"This is getting to be a habit."

"You wish."

At one o'clock, Gibb and Alicia sat down side by side at one of the desktop PC workstations in the Big Byte training room. Alicia handed Gibb the ham and Swiss sandwich and the soft drink she had brought for him.

"I've been meaning to ask you what it was like growing up in a place like Las Vegas," said Alicia between bites of her turkey sandwich.

"Very different from around here. My mother and I lived in a run-down trailer park bordering Westside—aka the black ghetto. Our neighborhood was called *the war zone*—high crime—drugs—lots of police activity. Not a place you'd ever have visited if you lived in Vegas."

"All I know about Las Vegas is what I've seen in the movies and on TV."

"*The war zone* might as well have been a million miles from *the Strip. The Strip* is what the natives call Las Vegas Boulevard where all the big hotels are located. That's the part of Las Vegas they're referring to when they describe Vegas as *the entertainment capital of the world.*"

"Were you into the drug scene?"

"What would you know about drugs?"

"During my senior year at college, some of my friends and I ran a soup kitchen in New Haven."

"Drugs never interested me—too many DOAs in *the war zone.* Malt liquor and street fights were my specialties during my hoodlum years."

"You certainly don't look like a hoodlum."

"Back then, all I ever wore were tight black pants, cowboy boots, and flashy shirts open to here," said Gibb, pointing to his navel, "so I could show off my gold chains."

Alicia winced.

"How did you ever get from there to here?"

"I was captain of the Bishop Gorman basketball team. After we won the state championship two years in a row, the coach got me an athletic scholarship to the University of Portland. When we first met, my rich roommate was so afraid of drive-by shootings he lent me the money for Levi's and a pair of hiking boots—it was all down hill after that."

Alicia pointed to the Polo emblem on Gibb's shirt.

"When did you meet up with Ralph Lauren?"

"That came later."

"Gerry said something about you're having gone back to Las Vegas after college."

"A week after I graduated, my mother died of cancer. She never even told me she was too sick to work anymore, or that she'd spent the last of her savings on her plane ticket to Portland to be at my graduation or that she was about to be evicted. The last thing she said to me was that I should quit worrying about her and concentrate on finding a job that paid really well, so I'd never find myself living in a trailer park again."

Alicia looked like she was close to tears. She reached out and placed a hand on Gibb's shoulder.

"That's a really sad story."

Determined to put the sad story behind him, Gibb continued on.

"I was so depressed, I decided to say the hell with it. My ex-girlfriend got me a job parking cars at one of the strip hotels for four thousand a month in tips. After that, I cleaned out my mother's things from the house trailer and rented an apartment near the Strip and got lost for a few years."

"What do you mean by *getting lost?*"

"Like the song says."

"What song?"

"Cigarettes, whiskey and wild, wild, women," said Gibb in a singsong manner, imitating Willie Nelson's voice, "they'll drive you crazy, they'll drive you insane."

"But you don't smoke."

"Not since my college roommate came and rescued me."

"And Gerry says you don't drink whiskey."

"Ditto."

"And the wild, wild, women part?"

"A lot less true than it was back then. Now it's your turn to confess."

"I'm tired of the spoiled rich girl label. I can't wait to break out of this town."

"Where will you go?"

"After I finish law school, I'm applying for a job as a prosecutor in the U.S Attorney's Office in New York or San Francisco."

"Speaking of this town—would you mind telling me how come the natives are so unfriendly?"

"They don't trust strangers—and I doubt they ever will."

"That's what Art Donovan keeps telling me."

"Art should know. He's been here for ten years and people still treat him like an outsider."

"He claims, unless you've been here for three generations, you don't count for anything."

"That wouldn't be far off the mark."

"For someone like me, attitudes like that take a lot of getting used to. In Vegas, it doesn't matter whether you've been there for five minutes or fifty years. The only thing that counts is how much money you have. Same as in any poker game, you can buy your way in. Those are a lot better odds"

A Northeaster was blowing in off Long Island Sound on the night Art Donovan called Gibb and said it was time the two of them got together at the hotel bar for a beer. They elected to go in one car. After dropping off his last fare, Art picked up Gibb at the Big Byte and drove to the Chatham Beach Hotel. He maneuvered his taxi into a parking space where the layer of slush and snow was the thinnest. Gibb sat beside him in the passenger seat zipping up his fleece lined suede jacket tight against his scarf and putting on his woolen navy watch cap. Mixed snow and sleet swirled around the outside of the car, obscuring their view of the dark grey swells crashing against the jetty and pounding the beach.

With the wind to their backs, they dashed for the side door, passing two rows of parked vehicles, their windshields encased in ice. It was the middle of March, a time when the hotel's unpainted shingles were as dark as they ever got, a time when the hotel showed its age badly.

Art was the first one inside. He stood in the foyer, wiping his feet on the straw mat, simultaneously shaking snow from his worn overcoat. Instinctively, his eyes scanned the bar area. The Regulars had their hats pushed to the back of their heads and their chapped hands closed around mugs of beer and shot glasses filled with cheap whiskey from the well. Foul weather gear of all sorts hung from the large wooden pegs on the wall opposite them. The mood was quiet. It was as if the Regulars were riding out the last of the winter storms, waiting for spring to make outdoor work bearable again.

Art led the way to the bar. The two of them sat on stools at the far corner out of earshot of the Regulars. Ignoring the hostile looks from the Regulars, Gibb waved to Sally Kilgore and called out their orders for hamburgers. Without waiting to be asked, Mark Hogan poured two mugs of draught beer. He set them down on coasters in front of Art and Gibb.

"How come the Regulars don't treat you like one of the boys?" Gibb asked Art.

"Cuz I was raised in a three-decker in Bridgeport—and that makes me shanty Irish. In this town, they never let you forget where you're from."

"I guess they feel the same about trailer park trash like me."

"When you're from a place like Vegas—it don't matter to them what kind of a neighborhood you grew up in. As far as they're concerned guys from Vegas are nothing but hustlers."

Smitty appeared at Gibb's side. Gently he tapped Gibb on the shoulder. Gibb turned and greeted him with the brother's handshake. Smitty's grin reached from ear to ear.

"You think I could learn to work one uh dem computers of yours, Mr. Gibb?"

"All it takes is for you to come by the Big Byte store on Sunday."

Art stared at Gibb over his glasses.

Smitty burst into a smile.

"Gee! Thanks Mr. Gibb."

Sally called to Smitty to clear the dirty dishes from a nearby table. Smitty shuffled away. Art frowned at Gibb.

"How in hell you supposed to teach a retarded kid to operate a computer?"

"You're way behind the times, Art. These days they have all kinds of educational software for that. It's even being used in the schools."

Sally came up behind them and put her arms around Gibb's waist.

"As if it isn't bad enough him being from Vegas," said Art to Sally. "Now he's plannin' to get hisself mixed up with a colored kid who can't even read."

Sally kissed Gibb on the cheek.

"I could care less—as long as Smitty doesn't start cutting into my play time. Besides," said she, poking Art on the arm, "the kid's a Catholic."

Art shook his head from side to side, disapprovingly.

"What's this I hear about Alicia Farrell being in the store again today?" Sally asked in a stage whisper.

"Sales are up," said Gibb, defensively.

"That better be all that's up," said Sally, pointing to Gibb's crotch.

Laughter from the Regulars rippled the length of the bar. A group of patrons seated in the dining room called out for Sally. Sally picked up her tray. She moved away from the bar, swinging her hips in her usual provocative manner. Art took hold of Gibb's shoulder. Pulling Gibb towards him, he whispered in his ear.

"Don't go getting any big ideas about the Farrell girl, or the judge'll nail your ass to a cross—and if he don't, you can be sure Old Man Bingham will."

Everything Gibb knew about power and influence, he had learned growing up in Vegas. In his home town, he was used to seeing it exercised in an upfront manner, frontier style. It was all about *juice* and there was no mistaking those who had juice from those who did not. In Chatham, he had seen scant evidence of juice being used to influence decisions of the Board of Selectmen. Occasionally the gossip mill buzzed about zoning denials and contract awards. But the cases in which the unseen hands of a Bingham or a Farrell were rumored to have intervened were mundane ones. They couldn't compare to the power struggles in Las Vegas.

"Give me credit for knowing better than to fool around with an engaged girl in a town like this," said Gibb, lowering his voice. "I'm not about to do anything that's bad for business."

Art surreptitiously pointed towards the Regulars.

"Every one of those guys thinks she's hot for your body. If they're right, you're in for a lot of trouble."

Snow was falling on Sunday afternoon when Gibb arrived at the front door of the Big Byte store. Smitty was waiting for him on the sidewalk, beating his arms against his sides, stomping his high-top sneakers against the pavement to keep from freezing. He was wearing a New York Yankees baseball cap, a present from one of the Regulars, and his white busboy's jacket was buttoned all the way up. Cotton clothing couldn't begin to protect him from the Northeast wind that had turned his lips purple and caused his nose to run.

Gibb greeted Smitty with a pat on the back, as he would have a shipwrecked cook's helper from a Bahamian freighter, which is what he imagined Smitty most closely resembled. Smitty grinned at him. The whiteness of Smitty's jacket and the snowy background contrasted sharply with Smitty's smooth black face. Gibb removed his gloves and unlocked the front door. He gestured for Smitty to move inside. Smitty failed to respond. Gibb gave him a friendly shove. Smitty landed on the inside mat. Poised as if on a stepping-stone in a pool of water, he shook his head from side to side, worrying out loud about dirtying the nylon carpeting.

Gibb left Smitty frozen in place. Moving about the store, he switched on the lights and the coffee maker and turned up the heat.

"Don't worry about the carpet," said Gibb when he was finished.

Smitty ceased staring at his sneakers. His big round eyes scanned the rows of computers and the shiny grey walls and the digital wall displays. A look of wonderment spread across his face.

"This must be a nice place to work," he said, at last.

Gibb led Smitty to a desktop PC at the back of the store. Smitty approached the PC as one would an altar in the Temple of Doom. Gibb had to coax him into the chair in front of the keyboard.

"This computer is people-friendly," said Gibb in a soothing voice to his skeptical pupil. "It's very easy to operate."

Smitty reached out and ran a hand over the keyboard. Gibb switched on the PC. The screen lit up. Smitty rapidly withdrew his hand.

"What happens now, Mr. Gibb?" asked Smitty, anxiously, his eyes widening.

"You're about to go back to school."

"Ah never did any good at school."

Gibb went to a nearby cabinet. He returned with a CD and handed it to Smitty. Smitty held the CD in his lap, examining both sides. On his face he had a quizzical look.

"What does it do?"

"It works the same as the ones that play music—only this one has a software program that teaches you how to spell words."

At the mention of the word *software*, Smitty dropped his chin against his chest and the CD in his lap. Gripping the sides of his chair with both hands, he locked his knees together and stared down at the CD, acting as if he had been stunned by a poison dart.

Gibb had witnessed sales prospects with far higher IQs react in a similar manner. He stood over Smitty, running his hands through his hair, worrying that Smitty was withdrawing out of reach. Smitty did not move a muscle. Moments later, Gibb was rescued by the sound of someone knocking on the front window. He was pleased to see Gerry Morgan waving her gloved hands at him.

Gibb dashed to the front door to admit her. She shook the snow from her fur hat and quilted coat and tossed them onto the nearest counter.

"How's the pupil doing?"

"He's frozen up on me."

Gibb led Gerry to the spot where Smitty sat motionless. She swooped in behind Smitty and covered his eyes with her gloved hands. Smitty's body remained rigid.

"Trick or treat?" she asked.

Smitty relaxed his body. Gerry dropped her hands to his chest. She hugged him tightly. Smitty raised his head. He smiled at Gerry, as if she had rescued him from a scary fate. Gerry moved around in front of him. She folded her arms like a schoolteacher. Leaning over him, she stared into his eyes.

"Remember how it was at St. Joseph's?"

Smitty grinned.

"It's just the same at the Big Byte, only here—instead of being called *teacher*—they call me the *Training Director*. My job is to teach people how to use a computer."

"I'm too dumb to learn anything."

Gerry picked up the CD from Smitty's lap and inserted it in a UB port.

"Nonsense. What we have here is a program called Ultimate Phonetics—"

At the mention of the program's name, Smitty recoiled.

"No need to be scared of the name," said Gerry. "It's as easy to use as watching the cartoons on TV."

Darkness was approaching when Gibb and Smitty piled into Gerry's car for the drive back to the hotel. Smitty sat shivering in the back seat, praying aloud for the heat to reach him. A short time later, they deposited him in front of the hotel garage and watched while he ascended the outside staircase to his room on the second floor. All the while, Smitty was whistling.

"You're the first yuppie idealist I've ever met," said Gerry with a smile.

"You're wrong on both counts."

Gerry poked Gibb in the ribs.

"You like to act tough—but underneath it all you're a real softie." Gibb's face turned crimson. "Which is why I'm beginning to believe Alicia Farrell does have the hots for you."

"You're as crazy as the Regulars. What would she want with me?"

"It wouldn't be the first time she's peed in the faces of people around here. That time when she set up the soup kitchen in New Haven, she teamed up with a couple of in-your-face lesbians. They dressed in fatigues and combat boots and wore their hair butch. She made the mistake of bringing them home for a weekend. They drove the town folks wild, holding hands and French-kissing in public and giving the finger to anyone who looked at them sideways. You can imagine how stressed-out her parents were."

"I still think you're nuts."

"Maybe it has more to do with people like Alicia wanting what they know they shouldn't have."

Chapter

5

Gibb and Gerry continued to give Smitty computer lessons on Sunday afternoons. What began as one hour sessions soon stretched into late afternoon, depriving Sally Kilgore of precious recreational time with Gibb. No longer were they able to watch the ball games together or spend time reclining on the living room sofa, listening to the local rock station and drinking wine and beer and exchanging stories about their experiences past and present and, lately, discussing the best courses for Sally to take at Gateway Community College during the fall semester.

Sally regarded her lost recreational time as irretrievable and she came to resent Gibb's inattentiveness. She complained to him time and again about being forced to pass the lost hours alone and unappreciated, smoking pot and drinking wine, wondering whether or not they had a future together. This she tearfully explained during a recent tirade caused her to conclude that his only interest in her was to satisfy his sex drive.

Having been raised by someone who was used and abused by her husband, at an early age, Gibb had promised his mother he would not grow up to be a user or abuser of women and he was stung by Sally's accusation that he was only interested in her for the sex she so willingly provided him. Nor did he believe that he was guilty of the latter offense. Understanding, as he did, that were the accusation true it would have placed him in embarrassing proximity to the space occupied by brutes like Mel Price, he protested his innocence, long and loudly. Despite his protestations, Sally remained unmoved and the debate raged on for several weeks.

Matters came to a head on a rainy Sunday afternoon in late April. Gibb returned from the Big Byte store to find Sally sprawled on the living room sofa, looking as though she had just returned from a call girl's convention. Dressed in a tank top and an obscene pair of mail order panties from the Frederick's of Hollywood catalog, she was smoking a joint and watching a porno movie on Gibb's Blu-ray Disc player. Women on their mounts were chanting the *F* word and moaning in unison, as Sally rubbed her crotch in defiance.

"What's with the porno flick?"

"You can turn it off," said Sally, slurring her words. "Mel and I already watched it."

Gibb seized the channel selector and turned off the movie. He threw the channel selector against the fireplace, shattering it into pieces.

"What the hell was he doing here?" he shouted.

"I called him up to ask him if he had any crack."

Gibb slumped down beside the fireplace.

"You know goddamn well, smoking crack will kill you."

"Only this time he told me I'd have to fuck for it—"

"He's as sick as it gets."

"So I invited him over."

"I suppose you were trying not to disappoint your mother?"

Sally gave Gibb the finger.

"Fuck you, Gibb."

She dropped her toke in the ashtray and gulped her wine. Gibb looked as though he was about to burst a blood vessel.

"How could you let that bum in here?" he asked through clenched teeth.

"I was totally horny and I couldn't think of anyone else to call," said Sally, sarcastically.

"You're talking like a cheap whore."

"Shows how much you know. Mel says I could get five hundred a trick, if I was willing to do the kinky stuff."

Gibb was getting angrier by the minute.

"Next time I see that asshole—I'll punch his lights out."

"Try it and you'll be dead meat—he's got a lot more muscles than you do."

"If you're talking about his brain."

"Since when are you such an intellectual? You self-righteous bastard!"

"There's no use talking to you when you're this far gone."

Sally drained her wine glass. Reaching under the sofa cushion, she pulled out her leather pouch and a package of cigarette rolling papers. She poured a small amount of pot on a piece of rolling paper.

"Haven't you had enough?" asked Gibb while Sally rolled herself another joint.

Sally looked up at him with a look that could kill.

"Instead of being so fucking critical, try explaining how an Irish Catholic boycotts Mass and then spends his Sundays trying to teach a black retard how to work a computer?"

"That's none of your goddamn business."

Sally's hand trembled so badly she had trouble lighting her joint.

"You wouldn't be trying to impress that blonde bitch you're so in love with, would you?"

Gibb sensed an explosion was near. He broke off the conversation and marched off towards the bedroom. Sally tossed the joint into the fireplace. Tears were streaming down her cheeks.

"Clamming up won't get you off the hook this time, Gibbsy. She's after your body and everyone in town knows it."

Gibb was infuriated by Sally's last remark. He yanked open the bedroom door and banged it shut behind him. The condition of his queen-sized bed convinced him that Sally was telling the truth about her having had sex with Mel. The covers were in such disarray, they looked as though Mel might have used them for one of his aerobics classes. Madder than ever, he tore his running suit from its hangar in the closet and began undressing. Images of Sally and Mel engaged in sexual gymnastics on his bed clouded his mind and placed him in a state of near paralysis. Moments later, the unnerving sound of glassware shattering in the kitchen broke his concentration. Dressed only in his underwear, he rushed back out of the bedroom.

Sally was pulling glasses from a kitchen cabinet and smashing them on the tile floor. She was sobbing loudly. Gibb stepped around the shattered glass. Grabbing Sally by the arms, he pinned her against the sink.

"For Christ's sake, Sally!" he shouted in her face. "Cut it out!"

Sally threw her arms around his neck.

"You've never loved me," she wailed, before breaking down completely.

"How can you even mention the word love—after you've spent the afternoon in my bed with that fucking pig, Mel?"

Sally pushed him away.

"I only did it to get even."

"And I suppose you think Mel will keep it a secret?"

"All you care about is what Art Donovan and the other assholes that hang around the hotel bar might say—you don't give a shit about me."

"I do give a shit about you, or I wouldn't have asked you to move in with me. The problem is, you don't give a shit about yourself."

Sally bent down and started gathering up the broken glass in her hands. She was too stoned to avoid gashing one of her feet. Blood spurted from the wound. Gibb helped her to a clear space and eased her to the floor. All the while, Sally was howling. He handed her a clean kitchen towel. With a dustpan and brush, he hastily gathered up the broken glass and deposited it in the kitchen trash container.

Sally wrapped her injured foot in the kitchen towel. Blood seeped through the towel in a widening pattern, dripping onto the tile floor. She stared at the blood and bawled. Worried about her loss of blood, Gibb dashed to the bathroom to retrieve his first aid kit. As he dressed her wound, she fell backwards against the kitchen cabinets and passed out. He picked up her limp body and carried her to the living room sofa. For the next ten minutes, he sat on the floor, leaning against the sofa, wondering whether the damage Sally had caused to their relationship could be repaired. The more he thought about it, the worse he felt.

Feeling the need to clear his mind, he finished dressing and set out on a long run. The weather was cold and overcast. For the next two hours, he turned over in his mind ways of improving Sally's outlook and boosting her self-esteem. He thought about offering to pay her community college tuition and about making time to help her with her studies. If Maria Martinez could make it out of the barrio to safety, then Sally could succeed in conquering her demons and arriving at a better place in life. Of this he was certain. His years in *the war zone* having left him with a soft spot for people who were raised on society's lowest rung, he felt obliged to try and convince Sally to cooperate in her own defense.

When he returned to Hampton Court, Sally's Volkswagen Beatle was missing from the parking lot. Nor was there any sign of her in the living room or the kitchen. Further inspection revealed that she had cleared the apartment of her belongings, except for her obscene panties. The obscene panties she had left in the bedroom on one of his pillows—out of spite, he assumed. His calls to her cellular phone went unanswered. Nor did she respond to the series of "*we need to talk*" messages he left on her voicemail.

The next chance he had to visit the Chatham Beach Hotel was after work the following Friday evening. Feeling the need for protection, he brought Gerry along with him. Art Donovan and the entire contingent of Regulars were crowded around the bar celebrating the end of a wet and miserable month of April. Their conversation was loud and animated. They were complaining about Sally having moved back in with Mel and about Mel having broadcast the news all over town. The Regulars were very upset about the news. To Gerry's trained ears, they were looking for a scapegoat.

Art slipped off his barstool. He caught up with Gibb in the dining room near the row of window tables. Pulling him aside from Gerry, he spoke to Gibb in a lowered voice.

"The boys wanna know how come you let Sally get back together with that bum, Mel?"

"All I can tell you is—it wasn't my fault."

"If you'd spent more time with her, instead of tryin' to teach Smitty how to read—maybe it would have turned out differently."

"We had a blowout last Sunday. She moved out. There's nothing more to it. I've tried to call her but she's not answering her cell phone."

"Chief's been in every night this week, trying to talk her out of it. He really has it in for you."

"If the Chief knew the whole story—he might not be so quick to judge."

"As far as he's concerned, the whole story is that you're after the judge's daughter and Sally isn't good enough for you anymore."

"Where do people get these crazy ideas?"

"From seeing Alicia Farrell going into the Big Byte every week. That's where."

"So I'm teaching her how to use the Windows 7 software program—so what?"

Gerry became impatient. She stepped between Gibb and Art and dragged Gibb away.

"Better be careful," said Art, in parting.

Gibb and Gerry took off their coats. They sat down at the window table the farthest away from the bar.

"What was that all about?" Gerry asked.

"Chief's blaming me for Sally moving back in with Mel."

"Caleb's a bad one to have against you."

"If he hates Mel so much, why hasn't he run him out of town."

"He's tried several times. But Mel's too popular with the corporate wives. Every time he gets in trouble, one of them steps in and bails him out."

The thought of Sally being back with Mel Price depressed Gibb. He stared out the window at the ocean. The ocean was full of whitecaps and surf pounded the jetty. No one witnessing this scene could doubt the accuracy of the predictions the Regulars were making about a late spring. Smitty came through the kitchen door. He walked towards a table full of dirty dishes a short distance from where Gibb and Gerry were sitting. Under his arm he carried an empty tray. He stopped short when he saw Gibb and Gerry.

"C-A-T spells cat, right Mr. Gibb?" he asked in a voice loud enough for everyone at the bar to hear.

Gibb's mood shifted. He smiled at Smitty.

"Right on, Smitty!"

Smitty swaggered in the manner of a person who was very proud of himself. Everyone at the bar laughed. Gibb stood up and exchanged fist bumps with Smitty. Smitty drifted away.

Sally appeared at their table. Without once looking at Gibb, she took their orders. Gibb felt very awkward. He was feeling sorry that he had talked himself into coming to the hotel. Sally acted as though Gibb had insulted her. She was scowling as she walked away.

"What came between you two?" Gerry asked.

"You don't want to know."

"Mel's been telling people you beat her up."

"Who'd listen to a drug dealer?"

"Caleb Nickerson."

The side door opened. Gibb and Gerry watched the chief and one of his deputies enter, acting as if they were on patrol. They went directly to the bar. Sally saw them coming and poured two mugs of freshly made coffee.

She laid the mugs on the bar on coasters and waited for the chief and his deputy to claim them.

The chief got there first. Taking off his service cap, he laid it down alongside his coffee mug. His deputy did the same. He greeted the Regulars first, then Mark Hogan. Mark nodded towards Gibb. The chief turned and scanned the area of the room where Gibb and Gerry were sitting. When his eyes located Gibb, he scowled.

"Speaking of the chief," said Gerry.

The chief swaggered over to their table. He stood facing Gibb with his hands on his hips and his feet spread apart, looking like he was about to issue a speeding ticket. Gibb looked up at him. The chief's eyes narrowed.

"I've been hearing bad reports about you."

"You must have me mixed up with some other guy," said Gibb. "I've been minding my own business."

"You'd better be telling the truth—because Vegas wise guys aren't welcome around here."

Gibb pushed his chair back and started to stand up. Suddenly all conversation at the bar stopped. Shaking her head sideways in a warning sign, Gerry reached across and grabbed Gibb's arm. Gibb got the message. He remained seated. Gerry turned towards the chief.

"Aren't you being a little rough on him, Caleb?"

"When I decide to play rough, your boss'll know it."

The chief turned on his heel and marched back to the bar.

Gerry tugged on Gibb's arm.

"If Caleb and Judge Farrell decide to team up against you—they'll run you out of town."

Chapter

6

G ibb no longer frequented the Chatham Beach Hotel bar. His visits to the hotel were limited to picking up Smitty before his computer lessons and dropping him off afterwards. Most of the nights when he was not out of town making sales calls, he resorted to eating frozen TV dinners cooked in his microwave oven. Occasionally, Gerry invited him to her house for dinner with her widowed mother. The only time he saw Art Donovan was when Art passed him in his taxi while Gibb was out running, or on those few occasions when he visited Art at his taxi stand opposite Bingham's hardware to exchange gossip. During his most recent visit to the taxi stand, Art spoke about Sally being seen riding on the back of Mel Price's Harley and about Sally missing work often and about how much Mark Hogan and the chief worried about her. Art's inside source at the health club reported to him that Sally was on a downhill slide. She was rumored to be smoking crack cocaine a lot and looking increasingly unhealthy. Art said that on the two occasions he had urged her to seek help, she told him to mind his own goddamn business.

Gibb became so alarmed, on a recent weekday evening he placed a telephone call to Mel's apartment to try and reason with her. Sally ended their conversation by telling him how great it was to be back in bed with a real stud and then cutting him off before he could respond. Shortly after that distressing encounter, Gibb telephoned Gerry at home to ask for her advice.

"What did you do to her to make her hate you so much?"

To Gibb's surprise, word had not gotten around town about Sally having had sex with Mel in his bed. Nor had Gibb mentioned the embarrassing incident to anyone.

"The day she moved out, she was ranting about how I'd lost interest in her. She was convinced the only reason why I was spending my Sunday afternoons with Smitty was to impress Alicia."

"Sally's not the only one who thinks that way."

"With Alicia spending her weekends with Josh Jr. in New Haven and with her headed there in September, it shouldn't be long before the rumor mill quiets down. Truth is, I don't give a damn what people are saying about me. I'm more interested in figuring out a way to get Sally to quit hanging out with Mel. The best thing for her would be to start taking courses at Gateway—and quit wasting her life smoking crack—before it's too late."

"The next time I see her at the hotel—I'll try to talk to her. But do you mind telling me why you're so interested in straightening her out?"

"Because she reminds me of the girls from the neighborhood I grew up in. So few of them made it out. Most of them became drug addicts and hookers. Drunken mother or no drunken mother—Sally doesn't have to end up in the toilet."

"I'll do my best."

Gibb no longer had any hope of reaching Sally. He left it to Gerry to try and convince Sally to break up with Mel. Business had grown to the point where his store was the leader in sales per square foot in all of Connecticut. The referrals he received from the Farrells and the additional sales those referrals generated from the town of Chatham and from the New Haven County government and from the county school system allowed him to spend a lot more time at the office, pretending he was intent on operating within his assigned sales territory. Corporate headquarters was so pleased with his performance and the example it set for the entire Boston Regional Office that his patron called and offered him the manager's position at the company's flagship store in Seattle, placing him first in line to become the next Northwest Regional Manager.

Gibb declined his patron's offer, his excuse being that his work in Connecticut was not yet finished. The GM indulged Gibb, because Gibb's performance had moved him back into the top rank of the Big Byte sales force. On more than one occasion, Gibb sought advice from Tim Perkins about his situation. Each time, Tim advised him forget about Alicia and come back to Seattle where the natives would again welcome him with open arms. Unfortunately, Gibb was now a fool for love—an affliction rendering him incapable of making a rational decision about his career.

In May, the weather gods smiled on Connecticut. They delivered to the townspeople of Chatham a series of sunny days, thawing their spirits and putting them in the mood for summer. Parks and Recreation Department workers were everywhere in evidence, cleaning up the flotsam and jetsam from the beaches, planting flowers and repainting the bandstand in anticipation of the summer tourist trade. Down at the town pier the annual repair work was under-way and there were stirrings at the Chatham Yacht Club.

On a Friday morning on one of the nicest days in May, Gibb was in his office pouring over his latest set of sales and inventory printouts when his attention was diverted by a commotion in the store. Before he could get out from behind his desk, short, officious looking George Collingwood III was standing before him, in his right hand holding a thin attaché case. Dressed in a seersucker suit and polka dot bow tie, Collingswood III's round, horn-rimmed glasses and his dour expression gave him the appearance of an old-fashioned head-master at a New England boarding school.

Gibb pushed away from his desk. Getting to his feet, he extended a hand to Collingswood III.

"Aren't you rushing the season a bit, George?"

Collingswood III was so taken aback, he refused to shake hands.

"I don't need a twit from Las Vegas to tell me how to dress," he said in an exasperated manner.

"I didn't realize Chatham was on your inspection list."

In choosing to arrive unannounced, Collingswood III had violated the company manual's eighth commandment. With Gibb's sales at record levels, he was especially irritated at Collingswood III's attitude. Before offering Collingswood III his spare chair, he flashed past him a warning signal at the employees hovering in the vicinity of his doorway.

"I'm not here on company business," said Collingswood III, settling into the chair in front of Gibb's desk. "I was in New Haven and I decided to take a little detour to visit with family friends in Chatham."

"Anyone I know?"

"I doubt it—they're rather prominent socially."

Gibb laughed out loud at Collingswood III's pretentiousness.

"It has to be either a Farrell or a Bingham—they're the only ones important enough to interest you."

Color rose in Collingswood III's cheeks. He placed his attaché case on Gibb's desk and crossed his legs.

"If you must know—it's Joshua Bingham Sr.," said Collingswood III in the same superior manner. "However, I'd much rather discuss why you turned down Corporate's offer to transfer you back to Seattle?"

"This town is beginning to grow on me."

Leaning back in his chair, Collingswood III stared at the Polo emblem on Gibb's button-down shirt.

"You may fit in well with the polyestered peasantry in this town, but rest assured Ralph Lauren isn't enough to get you through the door at the Chatham Yacht Club. The Yacht Club is one place that still believes in standards."

"You think like a Neanderthal, George."

Collingswood III stood, picked up his attaché case, and started out the door of Gibb's office.

"I think like a Bostonian, Quinn," he said over his shoulder, "which is something someone from Las Vegas is incapable of understanding. However, now that you're making an effort to stay within your sales territory, there is no reason why we can't co-exist."

"Make way for George the Third!" said a voice from the supply room.

"Disrespectful working class twit," said Collingswood III.

"Gerry Morgan can give you directions to Joshua Bingham's place," said Gibb to Collingswood III's back. "She's a friend of the family."

Gibb stood in the doorway to the file room. He watched while Gerry accompanied Collingswood III to his rental car. In the few minutes that Gerry was out of the store, there was much buzzing among the staff about the imperious ways of George the Third.

Gerry was frowning when she returned.

"Three and a half years later and he hasn't changed one bit," said she to Gibb.

"How does George the Third know the Binghams?"

"Supposedly, his father and Ezra Bingham were old friends. The way he tells it—in their college days the two of them competed for the Ivy League squash championship."

"I sure hope their conversation doesn't get around to me."

"Don't flatter yourself—Josh Sr. wouldn't know you if he tripped and fell down on top of you."

Over Gerry's shoulder, Gibb saw Alicia Farrell's convertible easing into a parking space in front of the Big Byte. The top was down. Alicia was wearing a pair of designer sunglasses. The sunglasses made her look like a movie star. She paused to insert quarters in the parking meter. Gibb gazed past Gerry at Alicia's pink button-down shirt and Madras jacket. In her free hand she held a brown paper bag.

Gerry turned and followed Gibb's line of sight. She watched while Alicia entered the store and made her way towards them.

"A little sunshine to drive away the dark clouds," said Gerry, as she departed for lunch.

Alicia presented the brown bag to Gibb for his inspection. Gibb inspected the sandwiches. Bag in hand, he led Alicia to the training room. They unwrapped their sandwiches, placing them on the counter between workstations. Alicia handed Gibb a can of ginger ale. Gibb snapped open the top and took a sip.

"I understand you have Smitty reading."

"At about the fourth grade level," said Gibb.

"I'd call that progress."

"The credit goes to Gerry. At this point, I'm only a cheerleader."

"Heather Caldwell says Smitty worships you. Apparently, he tells everyone at the hotel you're his big brother." Gibb's face reddened. "No need to be embarrassed. Everyone needs someone to look up to."

"Even you?"

"Even me."

"Who's your hero?"

"I don't have one particular hero. The people I most admire are the ones who are willing to risk their lives or their careers to save others—without looking for a reward."

"Courage under fire!"

"Right. And it doesn't have to be physical courage. To me, moral courage—standing up for what's right—counts just as much."

"This is one subject where we definitely think alike."

Alicia placed her sandwich on the counter and looked down at her lap. She acted as though she had just received some bad news.

"Is there something wrong?" asked Gibb.

"Josh has accepted a summer clerkship with a law firm in San Francisco."

"When does he leave?"

"In about two weeks. Right after final exams."

"Where does that leave you?"

"Sad and lonely."

"Anything I can do to help?"

"You could go sailing with me on my uncle's yacht some weekend."

"Won't people talk?"

Alicia raised her voice several octaves.

"What I do with my personal life is my business."

"People in this town don't seem to care much about a person's privacy."

"Because they spend so much time talking about you breaking up with Sally Kilgore?"

Never before had Alicia mentioned Sally to Gibb. Gibb wondered why she had chosen this occasion. He looked straight at her. She looked straight back at him. He wondered what she had in mind. His eyes shifted to her ring finger. A beam of sunlight caused her 4-carat diamond to sparkle. The diamond seemed to be flashing a warning signal.

"Because they're too damn nosey to suit me," said Gibb.

"Life is too short to worry about gossip. Besides— after I graduate from law school—I'm out of here."

Alicia's sailing invitation confused Gibb. In the past, except for the lone discussion with her about his mother, all they had ever talked about were the intricacies of the Windows 7 software program and how Alicia could make the best use of it to assist her uncle in his law practice. Not that Gibb hadn't made passing attempts at developing a more personal relationship with her. On each occasion, Alicia was the one who steered the conversation back to the safe harbor of computer programming. This had happened enough times to convince Gibb that once she decided to get engaged she had made up her mind to avoid engaging in any form of flirtation, even the harmless kind. So what was going on, he wondered? Could Gerry have been right all along? He decided a subtle inquiry was in order.

"From the ring you're wearing on your left hand, I assume you're still engaged."

"Your not suggesting this is a moral issue—are you?"

"I hadn't thought of it that way."

Alicia defiantly tossed back her head. She had the look of a teacher who was about to inform her pupil that he had flunked a final exam.

"I'll bet you hadn't."

"I didn't mean to offend you," Gibb said contritely.

With a wave of her hand, Alicia, brushed aside his apology.

"Speaking of moral issues—how come you spent four years at a Catholic college and you never attend Mass on Sunday?"

"How come you spent four years at Yale and you still do?"

Chapter

7

G ibb was up before dawn on Saturday morning. Dressed in his running suit, he slipped out the back door, bounded across his brick patio, and started off down a dirt path through the woods surrounding the backside of Hampton Court. He had spent a restless night reflecting on the previous day's conversation with Alicia, wondering whether Josh Jr.'s hold on her could be loosening. If it were loosening, he assumed that a summer's absence would give him ample time to test Alicia's resolve. And he also wondered whether this would be possible without feeding the rumor mill further. It was almost as though the townies had the Big Byte store under surveillance. After each of Alicia's visits, rumors drifted back to Gerry about what was being characterized as a clandestine relationship—one that was unseemly, if not downright immoral. Gibb became increasingly apprehensive about the damaging effect the rumors could have on Big Byte's sales pipeline. A feeling of uneasiness clouded his early morning outlook.

The dirt path led him in a westerly direction, connecting with the road that wound through the newer subdivisions where the split-levels and ranch houses were located. He looped around to the north of town, picking up speed as he entered the Boston Post Road at a point not far from Mel Price's health club. The Boston Post Road led him back to the town center where he moved passed the storefronts along Main Street at an accelerated pace.

Streetlights competed with the dawn light. Not a soul was stirring. He circled the town green and continued south past the Catholic Church to the turnoff leading to the town pier. A gentle breeze was blowing, cooling his cheeks amidst a scene so peaceful he was able to put Alicia out of his mind, completely. Ahead at the opposite end of a large paved parking area lay the pier. The pier was made of thick wood beams weathered by innumerable storms. Situated approximately a mile above the Chatham Beach Hotel, it stretched far enough out into the harbor to afford Gibb an unobstructed view of the Chatham Yacht Club and of an array of sailing yachts and power boats. Some of them were tied to moorings, others were riding at anchor.

Gibb slowed down to a walk. He circled the parking area several times before venturing out to the end of the pier. Except for a few fishermen with their long poles, the pier was deserted. He sat down, positioning himself with one arm wrapped around a piling and his feet dangling over the side. Gulls were silhouetted against the rising sun, diving for their breakfast.

At the sound of a boat horn, Gibb's eyes turned northward towards the vicinity of the Yacht Club. Searching the array of sailing yachts, he wondered which one belonged to Alicia's uncle. There were many of them for him to choose from. About half the number that the summer season brought, he had overheard one of the Regulars say. The sight was not unlike the ones he had awakened to mornings during the summer when he crewed for the Perkins on their family schooner, the summer that Tim Perkins and his father taught him how to sail. Until that summer, he had never even stepped foot in a rowboat.

He thought about having grown up in Las Vegas convinced he would die, if ever he were forced to leave the desert. In those years, the hot dry desert air had a powerful hold on him. The same could be said for the grandeur of the surrounding mountains and the smell of sagebrush and the lack of vegetation on the shores of Lake Mead. Reno was the only other city of any size he had ever been to and then only long enough to play in the state basketball championship tournament two years running.

Oregon had changed his mind about the desert. After being surrounded by lush greenery during his four years at the University of Portland, he no longer missed the desert. The lure of the ocean had released the desert's hold over him. When first he visited the ocean during the spring of his freshman year, the look and scent of the ocean had overwhelmed his senses and captured his imagination. So much so that, for a brief period of time, he considered putting out to sea on a commercial vessel. The ocean's magnetic attraction was what had kept him in Seattle for the past three years and the reason why the offer of a transfer to Chatham had appealed to him.

Were Gerry there with him, Gibb was thinking, she could have located Tom Farrell's yacht for him. In the brief time he had known her, she had become his expert on all matters having to do with the town of Chatham and its inhabitants. Not that he considered her outlook to be as provincial as most of the other natives he had become acquainted with. Although she hadn't ever been to the West Coast or seen much of the places in between worth visiting, she had been to Europe four times. She told Gibb she preferred old cities with grand cathedrals, which is why she spent most of her time abroad visiting London and Paris and Rome. Her father having been a successful businessman is what made her European travels possible. At the time of his death, he owned Chatham's largest insurance agency. And the amount of money he left Gerry and her mother was more than enough to pay for her trips overseas and for her to attend Albertus Magnus College in New Haven for four years without having to work. All this and more, Gibb had learned about the Morgan family during their frequent trips to the bar at the Chatham Beach Hotel.

The Dominican nuns at Albertus Magnus taught Gerry to take her religion seriously. She was, as a result, a true believer in the concept of Christian charity. This had a depressing effect on her social life. Too much of her free time was spent at the orphanage and caring for her mother and for underprivileged people like Smitty. And in an age when so many eligible bachelors were fixated on hard-bodied women, being overweight was a disadvantage seldom was she able to overcome. Gibb worried that she had resigned herself to a dateless existence.

At the University of Portland, other young women much like Gerry had befriended Gibb. Overweight, good-natured girls, one and all, they too had trouble finding dates. As a result, they became fixtures in the student lounge with a lot of free time on their hands. Much of their free time they spent teaching Gibb to play bridge—and correcting his diction—and in the evenings, cooking him occasional meals—and when Tim Perkins was unavailable, providing him with transportation to off-campus events. During his precipitous slide towards oblivion after his mother died, he lost touch with all of them. Thus, he was left with only one Gerry and he knew he would miss her if ever the rumor mill forced him to flee Chatham.

His thoughts were interrupted by the appearance of a freighter making its way along the horizon. He looked down at his watch. An hour had passed. He realized he would have to run faster in order to make his way through the downtown area before the first stores opened for business.

Minutes later, he had retraced his steps past the still deserted storefronts on Main Street and was headed north towards the turnoff to Hampton Court. At first, no cars passed in either direction. Then the fearful, ear piercing, unmistakable roar of motorcycle exhaust shattered the morning calm. Gibb had been around motorcycles enough to recognize the sounds were coming from a group of bikes bearing down upon him from behind.

In an instant, four giant Harley's were strung out alongside him. Turning his head sideways, he found himself staring at the scar on Mel Price's right cheek. Mel was dressed entirely in black. His black helmet was hanging from the handlebars. Sally sat behind him. Her arms were locked around his waist and her face was pressed against his shoulder. From the looks on their faces, Gibb assumed both of them were drunk or high on drugs. Recognizing trouble when face-to-face with it, he jammed both hands into the pockets of his running jacket and squeezed hard on his rolls of dimes.

Leather clad hoodlums all, the three other bikers pulled ahead of Mel. It was obvious to Gibb that they were looking for trouble and were pleased at having found it. Skulls were painted on the back of their leather jackets and their helmets were dangling from their *ape hangers* in the same manner as Mel's. Gibb could not imagine a meaner looking crew. He slowed to a walk and moved to the shoulder of the road, hoping for a passing car that would bear witness and scare them off.

The two bikers nearest Mel were big and ugly and potbellied. Both wore beards and hair down to their shoulders. Red and white polka dot bandanas were tied across each of their foreheads, completing the outlaw look. The skinny biker at the end of the line had his hair tied in a ponytail. The big bikers called each other *Animal* and *Gonzo* and they called the skinny one *Slim*. All three were swigging from sixteen-ounce cans of malt liquor.

In his youth, Gibb often had encounters with gang members. Each time, he had struck first without worrying about whether or not the threat was real. His habit of striking first in a bone-crushing manner had earned him a reputation for fearlessness and gained him the respect of the gangbangers who ruled his neighborhood. After he had battered enough faces with his rolls of dimes, he was allowed to carry schoolbooks in his backpack without fear of retaliation. Although the years in between had made him hesitant, he still retained enough street smarts to conceal his hesitancy from hoodlums like Mel and his biker buddies. In *the war zone,* hesitancy had cost more than one street fighter his life.

Minutes passed without any of the bikers speaking to him. After what seemed like an eternity, Sally addressed Gibb in slurred speech.

"Wanna go to a party, Gibbsy?" she asked through drooping eyelids.

The other bikers fell back in line with Mel. Seconds later, they came to a halt strung across the oncoming lane. Staring at Gibb menacingly, they swigged their malt liquor.

"If it's all the same to you, I'll pass," said Gibb.

Sally reached down and squeezed Mel's crotch.

"Easy, baby," said Mel, smiling a drunken smile.

"You know this queer?" the biker called Animal asked Sally.

"Yeah," said Sally, laughing. "I used to suck him off."

The other bikers laughed in an ominous way.

"Want us to work him over?" Gonzo asked Sally.

Before Sally could answer Gonzo, an oncoming car appeared from around the bend, forcing Slim and

Animal and Gonzo ahead of Mel. Gibb looked up at the sky and prayed for deliverance. Mel came to a stop a few yards ahead of Gibb, motioning for the others to line up alongside of him.

Gibb stopped and stared at the oncoming car. He was relieved to see that it was Art Donovan's taxi. The taxi came to a stop in the middle of the oncoming lane directly opposite the line of bikers. Art was wearing his summer straw hat and a faded green short-sleeved shirt with his T-shirt showing underneath. He rolled down the driver's window.

"Out for a ride?" he called to Mel.

Mel shouted back at him.

"None of your fucking business, you old fart!"

In an instant, Art was out of his taxi and raising his trunk lid. He reached inside for his soiled Army blanket. The blanket contained a .45 caliber pistol. Art unwrapped the pistol. He tossed the blanket back into the trunk. Slowly and deliberately, he crossed the median strip, with both hands holding the pistol steady, pointing it directly at Mel's head.

"Anymore smart-assed remarks from you and I'll blow your fucking head off," said Art in a loud voice. "And that goes double for your hoodlum friends."

Within Chatham Township, it was common knowledge that Art was a combat infantryman during the Korean War and had seen a lot of action. The look on Mel's face indicated that he was aware of these facts.

"We can take care of this faggot, anytime," said Mel, gesturing towards Gibb. "Let's move out before the old fart gets any crazy ideas."

The four Harleys roared off around the bend in the road.

Art shouted after Sally.

"You oughta be ashamed of yourself!"

Sally responded by holding high a wobbly middle finger. Gibb relaxed his grip on his roles of dimes.

"Did anyone ever tell you, that hat makes you look like Wyatt Earp?"

Art wrapped his .45 back in the blanket and closed the trunk lid. They drove to Main Street without exchanging another word. Art parked his taxi in front of the coffee shop. The two of them went inside where they sat at the counter and ordered scrambled eggs and coffee.

"Sally looks like she's strung out," said Gibb.

"She's just like her mother. Never had no self respect and never will."

"I was in love with a girl like her my last two years in high school. She was from the toughest neighborhood in town—and she turned out to be a winner."

"Yuh can't help someone who don't want help."

"Maybe so—but we've got to find a way to reach her. If she sticks with Mel, she'll end up in the morgue."

"You sound like you've got a guilty conscience."

"I've been thinking you were right when you said if I'd spent more time with her, instead of with Smitty, she might not have gone back to him."

"Talk to Gerry again—she's the only one I know has any chance of getting through to her."

✿ ✿ ✿

When Gerry appeared in the doorway to Gibb's office on Monday afternoon, Gibb was at his desk preparing a sales contract. Gerry was dressed in a skirt and a button-down shirt, looking as though during the weekend she had gained weight.

"My plane was late getting into Hartford Springfield. And before you ask—I'm starting my diet tomorrow."

Gibb stared at the dark circles under Gerry's eyes.

"You look tired."

"It was a long weekend."

"Meet any interesting people in Boston?"

"I ran into Collingswood III at a party on Beacon Hill filled with Harvard types."

"You're kidding!"

"I think he's gay. He was there with a psychiatrist who wore makeup and was very swish."

"Did he have anything to say about me?"

"He seemed pleased that Josh Sr. had never heard of you—although he did say Josh Sr. was aware Alicia's mother had bought the judge a PC from the local computer store."

"Hopefully, he won't be back for another three or four years."

"Not unless you start spending a lot of time outside our territory again. When he was in his cups, he said, if you did, he'd personally see to it that you were fired."

Gibb handed Gerry the sales contract he was preparing. Gerry read it slowly.

"Fortunately," said Gibb, "all Corporate cares about is the bottom line—and that's just what I've been working on."

"Thirty HP-PCs. It must be for the school system."

"Chatham High. The principal called me first thing this morning and told me the contract was ours, if I was willing to match HP's bid."

"Did you ask him how come they decided not to buy direct?"

"He said—from what he understood—it happened the day after Alicia's mother lectured the school committee members about supporting our local merchants."

Gerry looked at her watch.

"I've got to go," said she. "I have a class in ten minutes."

Gibb motioned for her to come inside.

"Shut the door," said he. "I have something I need to talk to you about."

Gerry's expression turned serious. The circles under her eyes seemed to deepen.

"Something going on between you and Alicia Farrell?"

"It's not about Alicia, it's about Sally. While you were gone, Art and I had a run in with her and Mel and some of his biker friends. She was totally wasted. We need you to help peel her away from Mel before she ODs."

"I'll try talking to her again."

"The sooner the better."

"How did Smitty do yesterday?" Gerry asked before leaving.

"It doesn't work without you—we played video games the whole time."

Gibb pushed away from his desk. He placed his hands behind his head and stared at the wall clock. He was worried about how much Smitty had come to depend on him. The computer lessons had caused Smitty's spirits to soar. Even the Regulars were impressed by the change in his attitude. They reported that Smitty was acting as though he had been awarded a college degree in English. In his free time, Smitty walked about the hotel carrying a newspaper under his arm, spelling words out loud for anyone willing to listen. He was so cheerful, all who believed in Christian charity were happy for him. Those not so inclined, including the chef and the chef's assistant, tended to look upon Smitty as a royal pain in the ass. They were, however, careful about openly expressing their regressive opinions because they were afraid of being punished by Heather Caldwell. Whether or not true, this was the version of the story Art had related to Gibb during breakfast the previous Saturday.

If the truth were known, Gibb was more uneasy about the potential fallout from his continued contacts with Alicia than he was about Smitty's increased reliance upon him. He worried that Josh Jr.'s departure for San Francisco would trigger another round of ugly specula-tion about his intentions, along the lines of—*When the cat's away, the mice will play!* If his analysis was correct, being seen with Alicia while Josh Jr. was away could hurt sales enough to cause his patron to order him back to the West Coast on short notice. His instincts told him that trouble lay ahead and he wanted to be free to move on without regrets and without having to look over his shoulder at Smitty's stricken face. These were thoughts better left for another day and time, or so he reasoned.

C h a p t e r

8

The jangle of the telephone at his bedside startled Gibb out of a deep sleep. Gerry was calling from Our Lady of Mercy Hospital in New Haven where she had assisted the paramedics in delivering Sally Kilgore. In a frantic voice, Gerry explained that Sally had been smoking crack cocaine continuously for a week and when totally paranoid had torn Mel's apartment to pieces. Mel was panicked enough to contact Gerry, begging her to get help for Sally.

Without the signature of Sally's next of kin, Gerry was having difficulty convincing the nun in charge of the psychiatric unit to admit Sally. She pleaded with Gibb to accompany Art Donovan to Bridgeport and help convince Sally's mother to come to the hospital before it was too late. Gibb hung up the receiver. He dialed Art's home telephone number. The telephone was on the table beside Art's bed. Art answered on the first ring.

"Who's calling?" he asked in a foggy voice.

"It's Gibb. Sally's in deep shit. Get over here as fast as you can."

A short time later, Art arrived at Hampton Court. Gibb dropped into the passenger seat of Art's taxi, slamming shut the door.

"Where too?" Art asked.

"Bridgeport."

"Why Bridgeport?"

"The paramedics picked up Sally and took her to Our Lady of Mercy Hospital in New Haven. Sally's strung out on crack. We have to convince her mother to come with us and sign Sally into the psychiatric ward."

"I wouldn't count on her mother helping her out— last I heard, she's drunk most of the time."

"If you ask me, Mel Price should be strung up by his balls."

"Let's face it!" said Art in disgust. "If it weren't Mel, it would be someone just as bad. Sally's been trying to kill herself for months."

They sped off towards the nearest Connecticut Turnpike entrance. The turnpike was engulfed in fog. Art travelled at seventy miles an hour behind a semi-trailer, hoping the truck driver could see the highway better than he could. The exit he chose led them into the ancient industrial section of Bridgeport. Gibb pointed to an abandoned factory filled with broken windows.

"I thought this only happened in the Rust Belt."

"Just when people around here started thinking it couldn't get any worse, along came the Great Recession," said Art. "They used to say you couldn't kill a dead horse, but it looks to me like they've managed to pull it off—what with the subprime mess and all."

Art glided to a stop in the middle of a street lined with decrepit wooden three-decker residences. On every floor, wash was hanging from clotheslines strung between the posts of outside porches.

"If my cousin Mike hadn't died and left me his taxi, I might still be outta work and squattin' on the front steps of one of these dumps."

"After seeing this slum, I don't feel so bad about the trailer park I was raised in."

"Now you know what Sally's all about," said Art, adjusting his straw hat. "Her old lady used to live on the first floor."

They got out of the taxi and walked up the front steps of the nearest three-decker. Art led the way through the front door into a mildewed entranceway. Above the first floor bell, the name *Kilgore* was handwritten in ink on a piece of adhesive tape. Art rang the bell several times. No one answered. Pushing open the hallway door, he motioned for Gibb to follow him inside. The paint on the walls was peeling and the hallway smelled like a garbage pail. Ahead of them a dusty staircase led to the floor above.

Art knocked on the door of the first floor apartment, quietly at first, trying not to awaken the other tenants. Hearing no response, he knocked louder and louder, until at last he could hear someone stirring inside.

"Whadda yez want?" asked a woman's gravelly voice from within.

"It's Sally's mother," Art whispered to Gibb.

The door opened a crack. Sally's mother was wearing a tattered housecoat and slippers with holes her big toes stuck through. The toenails were black and blue and cracked. Sally had told Gibb her mother was in her fifties. To Gibb, Sally's mother looked derelict enough to be in her seventies. She began coughing so badly, she almost convulsed.

"It's Art Donovan, Rashida. I gotta talk to you about Sally."

"Whose that wid yuh?"

"A friend of hers from Chatham."

"I heard about him. She get herself knocked up?"

"She's in the ER at Our Lady of Mercy in New Haven messed up on drugs. We need yuh to come with us and sign her in—so's the nuns can admit her to the psychiatric unit."

"Yuh ain't gettin' me tuh New Haven at this hour for that little slut."

"She really needs your help, Rashida."

"Well she ain't gonna get it. I didn't raise no daughter of mine to be no drug addict. She turned out worse than her bum of a father."

"We could go and get the cops. They'd make yuh come."

"In a pig's ass, they would!"

Shrugging his shoulders resignedly, Art turned to Gibb. Gibb pulled him away from the door.

"You wouldn't happen to have a pint on you—would yuh Donovan?" Sally's mother asked in a patronizing manner.

"I wouldn't offer you a drink, if you was dyin'."

"You never was any good—and yuh never will be," Sally's mother said before slamming the door shut.

Art and Gibb retreated to Art's taxi. Art switched on the ignition. He headed the car towards the Connecticut Turnpike. The two of them had glum looks on their faces.

"What do we do now?" Art asked.

"We drive to New Haven and try to talk the nuns into admitting Sally to the psychiatric unit without her mother's signature."

"On what grounds?"

Gibb settled back in the passenger seat and stared at the roof of the car.

"On the grounds that she's an orphan."

Art grimaced.

"You won't catch me lyin' to the nuns."

Art backtracked through the same run-down neighborhoods they passed through on their way to Sally's mother's apartment. The scene was so different from the impression of New England Gibb had travelled east with. He had envisioned a land of rolling hillsides and small farms and manicured small towns like Chatham. Nothing Tim Perkins had said prepared him for the sight of an old industrial relic like Bridgeport—with rotting interiors he had first viewed through the window of the Amtrak local during his train trip from Penn Station to Chatham. All the earmarks of urban decay were on display. To him, the rows of tenements and abandoned, multi-storied red brick factories with their broken windows were the grim face of poverty so unlike the mean streets of Vegas he knew so well. By the time they reentered the Connecticut Turnpike, Sally Kilgore made a lot more sense to him.

They left the Connecticut Turnpike at the first New Haven exit and made their way to Our Lady of Mercy Hospital. A few blocks from the hospital, Gibb called Gerry's cellular phone number to alert her that they were only minutes away. They arrived at the front entrance of the hospital at 6:30 a.m. The red brick building was located in a marginal neighborhood. It was very old and in need of repair. Gerry was waiting for them on the front steps. She hurried them inside for a consultation with Sister Mary Elizabeth, the nurse in charge of the psychiatric unit.

Sister Mary Elizabeth greeted them in the reception area. She was middle-aged and stout. In her nurse's uniform and her white wimple and veil and rimless glasses, she had the shiny-skinned appearance of a cloistered nun—one who took her solemn vows seriously. When speaking, she exhibited a patient, sympathetic view of the problems confronting the less fortunate. Her calm demeanor put Gibb at ease.

"You're certain her relatives are all deceased?" Sister Mary Elizabeth asked after listening to Gibb's earnest fudging.

"Positive." said Gibb. "We only checked around Bridgeport to make sure."

Art was standing behind Sister Mary Elizabeth. He winced while making an elaborate sign of the cross.

"Then that places her in the hands of the Sisters of Mercy. We've been overrun by crack victims lately—more fallout from the recession. Thanks to all the budget cuts, the police aren't able to do anything about it. I hope your friend Sally comes around. Some never do."

Gibb handed Sister Mary Elizabeth one of his Big Byte cards.

"Gerry and I work together. We'll help in any way we can. Sally Kilgore's a good person—she just got mixed up with the wrong crowd."

On the night all of the windows in Mel Price's health club were broken, there were as many suspects as there were seats occupied at the bar of the Chatham Beach Hotel when the Regulars were at full strength. This also was true when Mel's Harley turned up at the bottom of the harbor, about the same distance from shore as it would have taken had the Harley been pushed off the end of the town pier. Despite Mel's outcries, Chief Nickerson did not waste time investigating these criminal acts. To anyone who inquired, the Chief claimed they had to be the work of hoodlums from New Haven—probably, ones who had drug dealings with Mel.

Nor was anyone surprised when an early morning fire ruined the aquamarine carpeting at Mel's health club, nor at the extent of the damage caused by the ferocity with which Chatham's firefighters attacked the blaze. Mel complained long and loudly to the Fire Chief and to Chief Nickerson. Chief Nickerson responded by suggesting Mel would be better off relocating to New Haven where it was rumored people were friendlier to drug pushers.

According to what the police dispatcher whispered in the ear of one of the Regulars, Chief Nickerson's next visit was from a well-known New Haven criminal defense lawyer named Michael J. Vitale. Between cigar puffs, Vitale was rumored to have talked a lot about how the framers of the Constitution intended to protect the rights of legitimate businessmen like Mel Price. The Regulars were certain Mel could not afford to hire a lawyer as expensive as Michael J. Vitale. Therefore, it was not unreasonable for them to assume that one of Mel's clients had come to his rescue. This lesson was not lost on Chief Nickerson. He stopped hassling Mel and, whenever the townspeople complained, told them he had done the best he could.

By this time, the summer season was in full swing. The townspeople had no choice other than to turn their attention away from Gibb and Alicia towards the onslaught of tourists each year nearly doubling Chatham's population. Before ceding the bar of the Chatham Beach Hotel to the summer folk, the Regulars huddled together, passing judgment on the relationship between Gibb and Alicia. No longer did they believe Alicia was guilty of pursuing Gibb. The reverse was now accepted as gospel. This they concluded was what drove Sally back into Mel's clutches, causing her downfall. In their collective opinion, anyone expecting better treatment from a Vegas hustler didn't know much about Sin City. Gibb was now a marked man.

In season, Chatham was a very busy place. SUVs and minivans bearing Ivy League window decals clogged the business section and the access roads to the beaches on Long Island Sound. College students were imported to man the Yacht Club and the bar area and the dining room of the hotel. After hours, the college students patronized the beaches, drinking beer in great quantities and making loud noises until the wee hours. Their nocturnal activities annoyed the townspeople a great deal. Not however enough to demand their collective dismissal. The townspeople were practical New Englanders. They realized that there was a price to be paid in order to properly service the summer folk and keep the tourist money flowing.

Gibb watched the changes from the Big Byte's front window and from the sidewalk in front of the store, thinking up ways to introduce the summer folk to his computer offerings and praying for rain that would drive more of them inside. Busy as he was, he was unable to stop thinking about Sally Kilgore. Sister Mary Elizabeth's weekly phone calls kept him abreast of Sally's painfully slow progress. Crack cocaine had placed her in a state of near psychosis, one the psychiatrists at Mercy Hospital were having difficulty dealing with. Sally's belligerent attitude made matters worse. Gibb was aware that, had Gerry Morgan not been so well connected with the Catholic Church hierarchy, long since, Sally would have been transferred to the state mental hospital in Middletown and farther out of reach.

A few days before the Fourth of July, Alicia visited the Big Byte store. Wearing a business suit and eye makeup, she arrived unannounced. Her presence turned every head in the crowded store. Gibb learned of her arrival when he overheard Gerry calling out her name. To his surprise, Alicia bounced into his office and with both hands resting on the front of his desk invited him to accompany her to the annual Yacht Club dance.

"Let me guess," said Gibb. "The Yacht Club is trying to save money on the fireworks display?"

"Still afraid of what people will say—are we?"

"You have the luxury of seeing the world from the top down—at least this once, try putting yourself in my place and seeing how it looks from the bottom up."

"I'll take that as a no."

Alicia turned and stomped out of Gibb's office.

"If that's your excuse for being such a damned coward—I'm not buying it," she said over her shoulder in an angry voice, before slamming his door shut.

Gerry opened the door and poked her head inside. Gibb's chin was resting on his chest. He felt deflated and then some.

"Lover's quarrel?"

"She invited me to the Yacht Club dance."

"Let me guess—you turned her down." Gibb nodded affirmatively. "To the best of my knowledge, no one's ever tried that approach before."

"She knew damn right well, if I accepted, her family and the Binghams would find a way to drive us out of business—but that didn't stop her from accusing me of being a coward."

"You'd better get out of town for a few days and let things cool off."

Chapter

9

Gibb got out of the taxi at the 49th street entrance to the Palace Hotel in New York City and rolled his carryall inside. The sight of the ornate interior lifted his spirits, momentarily pushing aside all unhappy thoughts about Chatham. Tim Perkins had made the reservations at the corporate rate through his father's law office. On his frequent business trips to New York, Tim's father always stayed at the Palace, and Gibb's mention of the Perkins name brought forth a knowing—"*Yes, of course!*"—response from the desk clerk and a command to the nearest bellman to stand by for further instructions.

The high-ceilinged lobby, with its broad marble staircase leading to a section of the hotel that once was an elegant old Lexington Avenue mansion, reminded Gibb of the Fairmont Hotel in San Francisco. A few years before, Tim Perkins had taken him to lunch at the Fairmont on his birthday. He wondered whether Alicia would be staying there this weekend while visiting Josh—and whether together they would be watching the sun go down over the Golden Gate Bridge— and whether, had he accepted her invitation to the Fourth of July dance, she might not have made the trip. Determined to forget about Alicia for the weekend, he shook his head and concentrated on the good time Tim Perkins had promised him.

Tim was due in New York on a business trip for the Seattle bank where he was employed as a vice president. The previous week he had left Gibb a detailed voicemail message about the weekend *R and R* he had planned for them. The battle plan was a simple one. Tim had made arrangements to have dinner at the *'21' Club* with a girl he had dated while attending Exeter Academy. The girl's name was Heather Atwood. Heather was a Harvard College alumnus. Her friend Piper Wilcox—another Harvard alumnus—had agreed to complete the foursome. Heather was an editor at a fashion magazine. She had described her friend Piper as a good-looking young executive who worked as a commercial loan officer at a British bank.

Tim was certain both of their dates would be *fashionistas.* He strongly advised Gibb to dress accordingly. Gibb understood Tim to mean that he was to abandon Ralph Lauren in favor of the sleek Italian sport jacket and narrow legged trousers and dress shirt that Tim had talked him into purchasing at Nordstrom's and the Georgio Brutini loafers that he bought online. These purchases took place the previous summer when Gibb was flush with cash from one of his *Salesman of the Month* awards. At the time, Tim convinced him that, on their occasional forays to San Francisco, designer Italian clothes were guaranteed to attract their fair share of hotties.

Gibb napped in his hotel room until Tim had checked in and unpacked. They met in the lobby of the hotel dressed exactly as Tim had instructed. Tim was seated on a round velvet settee situated opposite the elevator bank in front of a display window featuring Oriental objects d'art. He wore his hair longer than Gibb and often was mistaken for a tennis pro at an exclusive country club. They clasped hands, and then slapped each other on the back, exchanging greetings in loud exuberant voices. Tim's boarding school accent echoed across the lobby.

The hotel doorman stood at the curb, waving at the passing cars until he was able to commandeer for them an empty taxi. Sutton Place was their destination. Ten months worth of gossip passed back and forth between them during their ride. The taxi driver discharged them in front of a mid-rise apartment building—one with a uniformed doorman standing at attention in front of its canopied entrance. The doorman held open the door, allowing them to pass through the entranceway into the polished marble lobby.

At the reception desk, a uniformed attendant instructed them to wait while he rang Heather's apartment.

"I'm glad to see Heather's father is still paying the bills," said Tim.

"What does he do for a living?" Gibb asked.

"He's a hedge fund manager—filthy rich, I promise you."

The attendant motioned for them to take the elevator to the top floor. The elevator discharged them into a carpeted hallway opposite a gold-framed wall mirror. They took turns examining their appearance in the mirror, buttoning the top buttons of their striped dress shirts, straightening the wrinkles in their jackets, and running combs through their hair. When finished grooming themselves, they thought they looked swell.

"Heather and Piper think you're from Seattle. So skip the Vegas trailer park routine and start acting like a Yuppie."

"You're telling me I should act like a phony."

"That depends on whether you're more interested in sex than sympathy."

Heather's apartment was at the end of the hallway. Tim rang the doorbell. From inside they could hear chimes. On the second ring, Piper Wilcox opened the door and introduced herself. A well-endowed brunette with a boarding school accent, to Gibb she looked as though she was ready to strut down a fashion show runway. She was wearing a metallic Escada strapless mini dress and Christian Louboutin crystal sandals. Gibb could not help staring at her. He was amazed at what he saw.

"Something wrong?" Piper asked.

Gibb blushed.

"No," said he, shaking his head from side to side in a flustered manner. "I was thinking about how hot you look."

"I could say the same for your outfit. I'm guessing Hugo Boss."

"Canali."

"Canali will do nicely."

Gibb looked past Piper at Heather. Heather was seated on the living room couch on the far side of the room. She greeted Tim and Gibb without getting up. Blue eye-shadow accentuated her black hair and white skin. Her choice of designer clothing was a Chanel black silk sleeveless mid calf shift topped with a cascade of black feathers worn with open patterned black stockings and, not surprisingly, Jimmy Choo shoes. And she exuded self-confidence. It was a scene F. Scott Fitzgerald would have appreciated. Thought Gibb to himself: *Tim was so very correcto when insisting that dressing Italian casual was the right way to impress these two hotties.*

On an antique hall table near the entrance, a bottle of New Zealand savignon blanc was open and packed in ice in a sterling silver wine bucket. Piper poured Gibb a stem glass half full and handed it to him. He declined Heather's offer of a joint. Heather apologized for not having a line of cocaine to snort. She said her supplier had been arrested the previous week. Piper claimed she didn't have any need for a supplier. Cocktails and fine wine were all she needed for a good time, or so she said. She was from Wilmington, Delaware—a place as foreign to Gibb as the Falkland Islands.

While Gibb's mind was at work adjusting to Tim's high society world and the thought that the good times were about to rock 'n' roll, Piper moved in alongside him.

"What are you thinking about?" Piper asked Gibb.

"How different this is from small town Connecticut."

"Heather said you're in computer sales."

"I manage a Big Byte store."

"What got you into computers?"

"I majored in computer science."

"I majored in French—but I wound up in banking."

"How'd you manage that?"

"Family connections."

"No shop talk," said Heather. "Remember?"

Back out on the sidewalk it was still light. Gusts of wind blew warm humid air in their faces. The four of them stood under the canopy waiting for Heather's doorman to hail them a taxi. The humidity made Heather and Piper uncomfortable. They worried aloud about their hairdos being ruined before the evening got started. Competing uniformed doorman were out in numbers, blowing their whistles and hailing taxis for the occupants of other apartment buildings on Sutton Place. Yellow cabs came and went in clusters, horns blowing in frustration, their roof lights unlit, until at last Heather's doorman managed to hail one for their group. Gibb was forced to share the front seat with an angry Iranian immigrant. Tim instructed the Iranian immigrant to take them to the *'21' Club*. The Iranian immigrant jockeyed his way over to Fifth Avenue in a hail of obscenities and screeched to a halt on 52nd Street, alongside the entrance.

Gibb got out of the taxi. Standing on the sidewalk, he stared at the metal grillwork framing the entrance-way to the famous restaurant whose laurels he had read about on the Internet and at the row of cast iron lawn jockeys adorning the balcony above the entrance. Piper took Gibb's arm. She led him through the entranceway and into the Bar Room. The Bar Room featured red and white checkered tablecloths and an array of antique toys and sports memorabilia hanging on wires from the walls and the ceiling. Tim and Heather followed behind them.

A waiter seated the four of them at a table against the wall. He handed each of them a menu. In examining the menu, Gibb exhaled noticeably. Tim laughed out loud.

"Gibb is not used to New York prices," said Tim to Piper.

Gibb shifted uncomfortably in his seat. Piper placed a hand on Gibb's thigh.

"Don't worry," said Tim to Gibb. "I have zee plastique. You can pay me back in installments."

Piper placed a hand on Gibb's knee.

"I promise you—I'm worth every penny."

Tim motioned for the waiter. He ordered a bottle of Mount Nelson sauvignon blanc. The waiter was impressed. He soon brought the wine. Twisting off the screw cap, he poured each of them half a glass. The sauvignon blanc set in motion conversation ranging from the Hamptons to Palm Beach to the Great Northwest to Europe and the Orient. Tales were told of summer travel, with but one exception, to places where Gibb had never been. The lone exception was Vancouver Island. Gibb had visited Vancouver Island on the Perkins' schooner the summer that he was a member of the crew. He was pleased at having something to contribute to the fast-paced stream of consciousness of his privileged companions.

The banter was light-hearted, the delivery unforced. There were animated descriptions of foxhunts and sailing races and polo matches and country club dances and international airports and luxury hotels and fabulous beaches. There was talk of stepmothers and stepbrothers and stepsisters and family fights over money and about who stood to inherit it and who didn't and all the reasons why. Gibb learned that Piper's mother had been married three times and her father four. One of her stepmothers even had been married to one of her stepfathers, albeit briefly. In Piper's rendition, life in Wilmington wasn't all Dom Perignon and foxhunts and debutante balls and laughter. Family feuds were plentiful. She said the feuds produced so much tension, she confined her visits to formal occasions—weddings and funerals and debutante parties, mostly.

The Atwood family background was a less complicated story—or so it seemed to Gibb in the version Heather chose to present. Some years before, her father had resigned his partnership at a Wall Street investment bank, moving to Greenwich, Connecticut to establish a hedge fund. His hedge fund made billions of dollars betting against the securities market during the subprime mortgage meltdown that almost destroyed the banking industry. Heather was very proud of fact that his willingness to gamble had made her father an icon.

Tim's family was normal by comparison. His forbearers were timber barons from Washington State whose wealth was enhanced by timely investments in software start-ups that turned into pure gold. Being the odd person out, Gibb felt defensive when Heather asked him about his family's business.

"My father lives in California. He owns a string of McDonald's restaurants."

"In this economy, those things can be gold mines," said Piper, enthusiastically.

"I haven't seen him in years. He divorced my mother when I was ten."

"Welcome to the club," said Piper.

Heather did not press Gibb for the details. She was more interested in being entertained by Tim. Tim switched to making fun of the stuffed shirts who worked at his bank in Seattle.

The wine flowed freely and the meal came and went and the four of them got along famously. So famously that when Heather and Piper excused themselves to pay a visit to the ladies room Tim leaned over to Gibb and in a low voice said it looked like they could have saved themselves the price of a hotel room.

Their next stop was one of the underground clubs in Soho. The club was packed with all manner of people, from the well dressed, to the undressed, to every manner of dress in between. Controlled substances were very much in evidence. Music pounded overhead. The dance floor resembled a snake pit filled with writhing bodies. At two o'clock, Piper leaned over to Heather and declared the party over. The foursome staggered back outside.

They parted company on a darkened street lined with old buildings with rusted metal facades. In the shadow of a doorway, Tim and Heather were busy undressing each other. Gibb managed to hail a taxi. Off he and Piper went to Brooklyn Heights, acting as though they were very much in heat.

They tumbled up the stairs of Piper's brownstone. The brownstone was situated on a hill overlooking Brooklyn Harbor. In the vestibule, Piper struggled with her keys. A few minutes later, the door opened wide, propelling Piper inside. Tripping over the doorstep, Gibb carried both of them down to the foyer rug in disarray. This was the moment when passion took an eraser to Chatham.

Gibb awoke to the jangling sound of Piper's cell phone. Half covered by a pink sheet, he was curled up in a corner of Piper's queen sized bed at the opposite end from Piper. Piper was under the covers talking in a muffled voice. After exchanging a few words with the caller, she passed the cell phone to Gibb and burrowed under her pillow.

"Have you by chance made arrangements for a late checkout?" Tim asked in a hoarse voice.

"What time is it?"

"Twelve o'clock—Prince Charming."

"Oh, my God!"

Wide-awake and stark naked, Gibb was starting to have second thoughts. He pushed himself up against the headboard and looked around at Piper's tastily furnished apartment. It seemed like fitting accommodations for a junior executive. The junior executive slid out from under the covers. She stood and made her way towards the bathroom. Gibb smiled at the sight of her lush pink body.

"Where are you?" Gibb asked Tim, absentmindedly.

"Still at Heather's. And you'd better be back at the hotel by two o'clock—that's the latest you can check out."

Gibb pressed the *end call* button. Art posters and Andy Warhol originals caught his eye. He was staring at one of the posters when Piper descended upon him wearing a short cotton bathrobe. She handed him a glass of orange juice and a vitamin B-12 tablet. Gibb was wishing Piper lived in Chatham.

"Do you ever get tired of one night stands?" Piper asked.

"It's been a while for me."

"Living in a hick town like Chatham—I'm not surprised."

"You sound like you know the place well."

"My last year at Harvard, I dated a Yalie whose family had a summer home there. We spent a lot of time hanging out at the bar of the Chatham Beach Hotel"

"He wouldn't by any chance be related to Josh Bingham? The Binghams and the Farrells are the only families who count for anything."

"As a matter of fact, he and Josh Jr. were close friends."

"You're joking?"

"So help me God—I read in the New York Times that Josh Jr. got engaged to Alicia Farrell. I promise you, Alicia is the only one who could get that professional Episcopalian to even think about getting married in a Catholic church."

Gibb was startled at hearing Alicia's name. He spilled orange juice on the sheet. Piper ran to the kitchen and returned with a paper towel. She began blotting in the vicinity of Gibb's crotch. Gibb was flustered, thinking of how small the world was and how easy it was to trip over one's self.

"Is there something I should know about you and the Belle of Chatham Township?"

"Not really."

"You wouldn't be planning to hit on her? Would you?"

"Why do you ask?"

"You're talking about someone who prides herself on being the last twenty-three year old virgin in captivity."

"Where does that leave Josh Jr.?"

"In a relationship straight out of the 1950s. He gets to stray—she gets to remain pure—and all's right in heaven. What more do you need to know?"

Piper's robe came undone. Gibb found himself staring at her nipples. Piper lowered herself on top of him. She smothered him with her lips.

"I have a two o'clock checkout," said Gibb, half-heartedly.

"If you lived here—you'd be home now."

Gibb barely made it back to the Palace Hotel in time to meet the deadline for checking out without paying for an extra day. Tim waited for him to pack and make his way back down to the lobby. Gibb checked his carryall at the bell captain's desk. Looking like they'd spent the night in hell, the two of them left the hotel and walked over to Fifth Avenue. They continued along Fifth Avenue—past St. Patrick's Cathedral—to the place where the side entrance to the Plaza Hotel faced Central Park. The Plaza Hotel sparkled in the abundant sunshine of a clear July summer's day.

They bought hot dogs from a street vendor and sat on a bench at the edge of the park.

"So you like Piper," said Tim after a period of silence.

"She's pretty cool," said Gibb.

"And she has awesome boobs."

"That too."

"And she'll cause you a lot less trouble than your Chatham princess."

"Quit preaching to me and tell me what I should do."

"Hang in there until your year is up. Then come on back to Seattle. From what you've told me, no matter how hard you try, you'll always be an outsider in Chatham."

Gibb was not surprised at Tim's advice. Where women were concerned, Tim hated complications. He believed in moving on the minute the good times came to an end.

"I see you haven't changed."

"And what's with you teaching a black retard how to operate a computer?"

"Who told you that?"

"I overheard you talking to Piper in that under-ground zoo in Soho."

"A little Christian charity. That's all it is."

"From a guy who won't even go to church at Easter?"

"How'd you like to be black and retarded in a place like Chatham?"

"On days like this, I'm not sure I'd know the difference."

Chapter

10

Had Gibb been asked to choose how he preferred to spend his free time during any particular Saturday in July, without question, visiting Sally Kilgore in the psychiatric ward at Our Lady of Mercy Hospital would have been his last choice. Unfortunately for him, during his last conversation with Sister Mary Elizabeth, Sister Mary Elizabeth had insisted that Sally's situation was growing more desperate every hour. That was the only reason he agreed to make the trip.

Gibb took a local Amtrak train to New Haven. He passed the time planning the following week's sales presentation to the county school system's procurement office and sifting through the wreckage of his relationship with Sally. Sally's inability to overcome her background continued to puzzle him. Girls from *the war zone* who had grown up and become hookers had higher opinions of themselves. And none of them were endowed with Sally's looks or intelligence. Most of them had mothers who were beaten regularity by their live-in boyfriends. Yet somehow they had managed to survive. Why not Sally, he wondered? Why was she so hell bent on destroying herself? Life was such a mystery.

He arrived at the New Haven train station in the midst of a driving rain. The cab driver that drove him to Our Lady of Mercy Hospital was of Italian descent. In every other respect, he resembled Art Donovan. He was a man of the same generation who wore the same kind of straw hat and flowered shirt and black trousers and white socks. He even had a Saint Christopher medal pinned above the rear-view mirror. Whenever he could, he attended Mass in the hospital chapel, asking God to provide jobs for his friends and relatives, especially the ones that the Great Recession had thrown out of work and that were unlucky enough to have exhausted their unemployment benefits.

"When the nuns are gone," said the taxi driver, despairingly, "I don't know who in hell's gonna look after the poor people around here when they get sick. I guess if those Tea Party people in Washington have their way, they'll all be left out in the cold to die."

Gibb sat in the back seat, only half-listening to the driver, trying to think of what he could say to Sally that might help lift her spirits.

Saturday was a busy day at *Mercy*—as the cab driver kept referring to the Catholic hospital. Mercy was a time-worn eleemosynary institution. Its walls were painted institutional green. Scarred chair rails bordered the walls; the corridors were lined with dark vinyl floor covering polished to a high gloss. Orderlies and nurses and interns rushed about caring for the crush of people the proprietary hospitals turned away. At the reception desk, the receptionist told Gibb to wait in the reception room for Sister Mary Elizabeth. The reception room was filled with working class people, watching a rerun on a television set suspended overhead, patiently awaiting treatment. Gibb removed his raincoat. He sat on one of the worn wooden benches lining the walls, wondering what to expect from Sally.

It wasn't long before Sister Mary Elizabeth appeared in the reception room. She was the same picture of an old fashioned nun Gibb remembered from his first visit. They exchanged perfunctory greetings.

"We have to hurry so you can visit Sally before her therapy begins."

"What is it you want me to do, Sister?"

"See if you can get through to her. Right now, she's too defiant for her own good. If she doesn't come around soon, we'll have to transfer her to the state hospital in Middletown—that place could turn her suicidal."

They took the elevator to the psychiatric unit located on the top floor. A digital lock secured the entrance. Overhead, round polished metal mirrors were set at angles for surveillance purposes. Sister Mary Elizabeth entered the combination to the lock. The door opened into the interior corridor. She led the way to the day room. The day room was at the far end of the corridor.

"You're apt to be shocked when you see her."

"Has she had any other visitors?"

"Only Chief Nickerson from the Chatham Police—something to do with a drug investigation. He seemed terribly concerned about Sally."

Gibb doubted that the chief was there on police business. From what Art Donovan had heard, the chief had closed the investigation and Mel was back peddling cocaine to the bored wives who frequented his health club.

"The chief treats her like the father she should have had," said Gibb.

Without warning, halfway down the corridor, Sister Mary Elizabeth came to a full stop. Looking over her rimless glasses, she pointed a finger at Gibb—like a schoolteacher might have. Gibb was taken aback.

"What do you know about Sally's mother?" Sister Mary Elizabeth asked with a penetrating look on her face.

Gibb glanced sideways, at the same time, raising his eyes towards the windows where a heavy rain beat against the window panes. The scene was very depressing to him. He assumed the good Sister knew Sally's mother was alive. It seemed pointless for him to lie to her, again.

"She's an alcoholic. Lives in one of the worst slums in Bridgeport and looks twenty years older than she is. We tried to convince her to come with us the day Sally was admitted. But she refused—said she didn't raise Sally to be a drug addict."

"She sounds like someone who's more to be pitied than judged harshly."

"She has less respect for her daughter than she has for herself."

"Perhaps, because her husband abandoned her."

"My father abandoned my mother, too. She never tried to get even with him by calling me a bum."

"Hard times can cause people to say things they don't mean."

Gibb felt like he was in the presence of Mother Theresa. The urge to argue drained out of him. Forgiveness for Sally's mother was out of the question.

"I'm sure you're right," said he, as sincerely as he knew how.

Sister Mary Elizabeth smiled approvingly.

"A little Christian charity goes a long way."

They entered the day room. The day room had the worse kind of institutional look. Chairs and plastic tables made of white vinyl were scattered about the vinyl flooring. The floor covering was the same dark color as the floor covering in the corridors. Magazines and board games were randomly placed on the tables. To Gibb's eyes, the room was the picture of dreariness personified.

Sally was sitting on a chair in the far corner of the room, resting her feet on a leaky radiator. She was staring out the window at the rain. Other patients were gathered in the middle of the room, their chairs drawn in a semi-circle around a color television set of ancient vintage. None of the patients seemed to notice how much the rainstorm was interfering with the reception.

Sister Mary Elizabeth guided Gibb to the place where Sally was sitting. Sally was dressed in a blue hospital robe. She was wearing fuzzy pink slippers. She did not acknowledge their presence. Sister Mary Elizabeth gently placed a hand on her shoulder.

"You have a visitor, Sally," she said cheerfully.

Sally turned sideways. As if in a trance, she stared at Gibb, blankly. Her cheeks were sunken. Under her eyes, there were deep, dark circles. Gibb was shocked at her emaciated appearance. She looked to him like a victim of a Nazi concentration camp.

"Hello, Sally!" he said nervously.

Sally's eyes opened wide.

"What the fuck are you doing here?" she asked in a loud voice.

Gibb was so embarrassed he was struck dumb.

"No need to be embarrassed on my account. Sally doesn't realize what she is saying."

"The fuck I don't. For all I care, you can take these slippers the chief brought me and shove them up your virgin ass."

Sister Mary Elizabeth began backing away from them.

"I'll leave you two alone," said she gently. "I'm sure you have a lot to talk about."

"Shows how much you know—you old fart. We don't have a fucking thing to talk about."

"Calm down. You have therapy in an hour."

"For your info, I'm sick of therapy. And sick of everything else that goes on in this prison."

Sister Mary Elizabeth disappeared into the corridor. Gibb pulled up a chair alongside Sally. He sat down and placed a hand on her thigh, attempting to comfort her. Sally turned back towards the window. She resumed staring at the rain. Moments later, she folded her arms, sobbing uncontrollably. Tears were streaming down her face.

"Why did you have to come?"

"I wanted to see how you were doing."

"You're a lying son of a bitch! You're no better than that rotten mother of mine who signed me into this prison."

"It's not a prison—it's a hospital. State hospital's a prison—and that's where you're headed, if you don't snap out of it."

"What good would that do? There's nothing left for me."

"With a little cooperation, you could get out of here and go back to work."

"That's bullshit and you know it. No one wants anything to do with me."

"Of course they do."

"Oh yeah! Name one."

"Chief Nickerson."

"Only thing Caleb's interested in, is busting Mel for supplying me with crack. You wouldn't happen to have any with you—would you?"

Gibb was shocked.

"Are you crazy?"

Sally let loose a wild uncontrollable laugh. The other patients turned away from watching television and stared at her.

"Shut your face!" one of the other patients shouted at Sally. "We're trying to watch TV."

Sally waved a middle finger at the television viewers.

"I'll tell you one thing lover boy. If you're not crazy when you get here, you soon will be."

"You can make it, Sally. I know you can."

"Why did you have to fall in love with that Farrell bitch," Sally asked in a quiet voice.

"Mel tell you that?"

"I didn't need to be told. Once you got to meet her, I knew I'd never be good enough for you."

"It wasn't a question of being good enough."

"Have it your way. When you started staying away on Sundays, I knew we were finished."

"I wasn't staying away from you. I was just trying to teach Smitty how to read and use a computer. That was all there was to it."

Sally burst into tears.

"He started beating the crap out of me, Gibb. And he forced me into all kinds of kinky sex—wouldn't give me any more crack till I got it on with his biker buddies. Turned me into a fucking *mama*."

"Jesus, Sally! Weren't you worried about AIDS?"

"When you've sunk that low, nothing matters. Not even AIDS."

Sister Mary Elizabeth reappeared. She stepped between Gibb and Sally and patted Sally on the shoulder.

"I see that the two of you have had a nice visit. Now it's time for your medication."

Sally shrugged her shoulders. Gibb got to his feet. He reached for Sally's hands to help her up. Sally gave them to him without hesitation. Gibb looked straight at Sally.

"Promise me you'll try and get well," said he in earnest.

"I will, if I can have you back."

"You know how I feel about life. Anything's possible— if you put your mind to it."

Sally smiled. Her smile caused Sister Mary Elizabeth to beam. Gibb walked with Sister Mary Elizabeth and Sally to a room nearby. He waited outside while Sister Mary Elizabeth eased Sally onto a chair and made her swallow her medication. She sat on the edge of the examining table, holding Sally's hands, explaining how much easier it was for her when she cooperated. Sally rested her chin on her chest. She closed her eyes and nodded off.

Sister Mary Elizabeth stepped back into the corridor, gently shutting the door behind her. She escorted Gibb back to the entrance to the psychiatric unit. Not a word passed between them until she had unlocked the door and was seeing Gibb out.

"Thank you so much for coming," she said quietly. "You may have saved Sally's life."

Gibb stepped into the hallway. He started walking towards the elevators.

"God bless you," Sister Mary Elizabeth called after him.

Gibb experienced a rush of goose bumps. The goose bumps lasted all the way to the elevator. He was hoping he would never again have to visit a scene as depressing as this one.

Chapter

11

A week had passed since Gibb returned from New Haven. He had not heard any further news from Sister Mary Elizabeth. Seated at his desk on Friday afternoon, he was examining his latest salesman's call sheet when Gerry walked into his office unannounced and sat down in front of him. The scowl on his face signaled to Gerry that he was in an unhappy mood.

"What's wrong?" she asked.

Gibb handed her the call sheet.

"This makes five good leads in a row I've lost. Haven't had this happen since my first year as a salesman."

"Maybe it has something to do with Alicia coming back early from her trip to San Francisco. Rumor has it, she and Josh Jr. had a fight."

"What's that got to do with me?"

"Don't be so damn naïve, Gibb. Before she decided to visit Josh Jr., people were so worked up, they were ready to lynch you."

"Since when is giving computer lessons a crime?"

"Since the powers that be decided you've been using them to try and steal Alicia away from Josh Jr."

"Those people have vivid imaginations. Alicia hasn't spoken to me since I refused to go to the Fourth of July dance with her."

The ringing of the telephone interrupted their conversation. Gibb did not recognize the caller's voice. He was startled when the caller announced he was Tom Farrell. Had Gibb been asked in advance, he would have guessed the odds were a thousand to one against Alicia's uncle inviting him for a weekend sail on his yacht. In a state of confusion, he placed a hand over the receiver and spoke to Gerry in a whisper.

"Its Alicia's uncle. He wants me to crew for him this weekend."

Gerry was as surprised as Gibb. She raised her eyebrows in wonderment.

"I wouldn't bother you," said Uncle Tom. "But without a second strong hand aboard we'll be stuck in port for the weekend and all the usual suspects at the Yacht Club have other plans. Incidentally, Mary has a girlfriend in from New Haven. While you're at it, you can help me entertain her."

Gerry motioned for Gibb to again place his hand over the receiver. Gibb complied mechanically.

"You should go. Maybe Uncle Tom can help take the heat off you."

JOHN HENRY BREBBIA **141**

Gibb took his hand off the receiver and leaned back in his chair.

"In that case, count me in," he said to Uncle Tom, matter-of-factly. "I'd hate to be the one to spoil your weekend."

"Meet me at the Yacht Club tomorrow morning at seven bells."

Gibb hung up the receiver. Inhaling deeply, he slumped back in his chair. He had a puzzled look on his face.

"Am I supposed to know who Mary is?"

"That would be Mary Walsh—the head housekeeper at the hotel. They've been having an affair for years."

"What's a Farrell doing dating a maid?"

"Technically speaking, she's not a maid, she's a supervisor. Besides, they say she's a great cook."

"If you didn't know about this phone call, what would you say the odds were on Uncle Tom inviting me for a weekend sail on his yacht—let alone, fixing me up with a date?"

"A thousand to one?"

"Exactly what I was thinking. Aside from meeting him once when he dropped Alicia off for a lesson, I hardly know the guy. What do you supposed he's up to?"

"There's only one way to find out."

✿ ✿ ✿

At the sound of Art Donovan's car horn, Gibb bounded out of his apartment and hurried down the front walk. He yanked opened the rear door to Art's taxi and heaved his duffel bag into the back seat. Dressed in a plaid flannel shirt and khaki trousers and a worn pair of boating moccasins and with a yellow slicker tied loosely around his neck, he settled into the front seat. Art set off immediately for the Chatham Yacht Club parking lot. They arrived a few minutes before 7:00 a.m. Art parked close to the Yacht Club pier. He waited while Gibb retrieved his duffel bag. A series of cabin cruisers and small sailboats were docked along both sides of the pier.

The Yacht Club was situated on a point of land. On its backside, a small sandy beach stretched the length of the property. There was nothing distinctive about the building's appearance. It was—as Art had explained to Gibb—vintage New England—all the way from its unpainted shingles and blue trim to the large wooden deck overlooking the beach, affording a commanding view of Long Island Sound. The deck was covered by an awning in the same shade of blue as the building trim. It was strewn with white metal tables and deck chairs. To Gibb, the club seemed like an unlikely vantage point from which to look down upon the local popu- lace. Although he had heard stories from Art about this being exactly how its members usually acted towards the natives during the summertime.

"I'd appreciate it, if you'd keep your mouth shut about Uncle Tom fixing me up with one of Mary Walsh's friends," said Gibb before closing the rear door.

"Try not to fall overboard," said Art.

Gibb walked out to the end of the pier. Uncle Tom was standing in an inflatable dingy, waiting for him to come aboard. Until this moment, Gibb had paid little attention to the weather. The sun was shining and a spanking breeze was blowing off shore at fifteen knots. Whitecaps rocked the dinghy. Uncle Tom had to struggle to hold it in place against the pier.

Gibb handed Uncle Tom his duffel bag and climbed aboard the dingy. Uncle Tom was over six feet tall and angular. Beneath his yachting cap a prominent nose and large white teeth were his most pronounced features. His blue eyes were set deep in their sockets and his face was tanned from many days spent on the water. He had the serious demeanor of a combat veteran— according to Art Donovan—one who had commanded a Navy SEAL unit in the closing days of the Vietnam War. Dressed in a worn set of khakis, his life jacket hung loosely around his chest. Outwardly, the only thing he and Gibb had in common was that they both were wearing aviator sunglasses.

He greeted Gibb with a peremptory nod of his head. His look was stern and off-putting, not unlike certain Big Byte sales managers that Gibb had learned to avoid whenever possible. Gibb thought Uncle Tom most closely resembled one of those grouchy naval officers with rugged looks—the type pictured in vintage movies about the War in the Pacific. Before casting off, he instructed Gibb to sit in the front of the dingy and to hold on tight lest the white caps knock him overboard.

Gibb untied the sleeves of his yellow slicker. He put on the slicker and zipped it all the way up. Uncle Tom yanked on the cord of the small outboard motor. A puff of smoke escaped from the exhaust system. Off they went towards Uncle Tom's yacht. The two of them caught spray, motoring the hundred yards to the place where a white-hulled performance cruiser rode at double mooring. From the transom, the sleek 50-foot sailing vessel was flying the American flag and the flag of the Chatham Yacht Club. She was as pretty a sailing vessel as any Gibb had ever seen on the West Coast.

On the stern, above the inscription *Chatham Connecticut,* the name *Happy Ending* was painted in large gold letters. A woman Gibb presumed to be Mary Walsh was standing in the cockpit. Through her red spandex top, her nipples were clearly visible. She had auburn hair and green eyes and a pleasing, freckled Irish face. Gibb judged her to be in her late thirties, much younger than Uncle Tom. Nowhere in sight was her friend from New Haven.

Uncle Tom brought the dinghy alongside the transom ladder. He held it fast while Gibb climbed aboard, carrying his duffel bag over his shoulder.

"I'm the captain's wench," said Mary, extending a hand over the side to Gibb.

Gibb asked her where her friend was. Mary smiled at him.

"In the galley making coffee."

Gibb threw his duffel bag into the cockpit. Uncle Tom came aboard behind him. With the aid of the electric winch, Uncle Tom and Gibb hauled up the dingy and quickly deflated it. Uncle Tom fastened the outboard motor to its bracket on the pushpit, while Mary stored the dingy in the dingy garage below the cockpit.

"You can go below and stow your gear," said Uncle Tom to Gibb. "Mary and I will cast off."

Gibb dropped his duffel bag down the companionway. He descended the wooden ladder backwards, savoring the smell of freshly brewed coffee coming from the galley. When his feet reached the bottom deck, he turned around and was shocked to see Alicia standing with her back to the sink. Holding a mug of coffee in her right hand, Alicia was wearing a white turtleneck jersey and white pants and a Yale sweatshirt. At the sight of him, she smiled an engaging smile.

Gibb's mouth dropped open.

"Surprised?"

"More like amazed."

"You didn't think I'd let Uncle take you on an overnight sail without me—did you?"

"Honestly, I didn't know what to think when he called to invite me."

"We're all happy to have you on board."

"How's Josh?"

"I suppose you heard we had a big fight."

"Like you've often said—there are no secrets in this town."

"Why don't you stow your bag in the starboard forward cabin and join me for a cup of coffee while Uncle Tom pilots us out of the harbor."

Gibb picked up his duffel bag and started down the passageway.

"Don't you want to know what the fight was about?" Alicia asked over his shoulder.

"It's none of my business."

"It was about Josh leaving me in the lurch this summer— when he could just as easily have clerked in New York."

Gibb paused. He made a half turn toward Alicia.

"I take it this is your way of telling me you invited me to get even."

"That's one way of looking at it."

Alicia was in the midst of recounting her first impressions of San Francisco when Uncle Tom shouted down the companionway the *"All hands on deck!"* command. The Happy Ending had cleared the harbor and it was time to hoist the sails. Gibb and Alicia dropped their coffee mugs in the sink. Clamoring on deck, they set about hoisting the mainsail and then the staysail and the Yankee. A spanking breeze soon had the staysail and the Yankee billowing in the wind.

With the vessel underway, they returned to the cockpit and joined Mary in gathering round while the skipper issued the day's standing orders. Uncle Tom's plan was to sail as far to the east as possible before turning back towards Barrows Point on the eastern tip of Long Island where he had reserved a berth for the night. In rotation, the crew members were to take one-hour turns at the wheel—Uncle Tom first, then Mary, then Gibb, then Alicia.

After a round of *aye, aye, sirs!* Alicia and Gibb made their way along the side-deck to the pulpit. For the next two hours, they sat with their backs against the cabin trunk, their arms locked around their knees, welcoming spray and engaging in small talk about seagulls and marine life and landmarks in the order in which they came into view. Alicia seemed perfectly content—so content, Gibb allowed himself the luxury of thinking there might be room for him in her future.

At 1030 hours, Mary handed over the wheel to Gibb and followed Uncle Tom below deck. Other than when announcing the day's standing orders, Uncle Tom had spoken but a few words in Gibb's presence. According to Alicia, Uncle Tom regarded his sailing time as being sacred time. For Uncle Tom, it was time reserved for communing with nature, time away from the cacophony of cell phone chatter and from the ever present email and fax traffic and text messages all during office hours and often late into the evening, pressing upon him the constant demands of his wealthy clients. Gibb understood Uncle Tom's attitude perfectly. The sea had a similar effect on him. Banished from his mind were thoughts of Sally's plight and missed sales opportunities and of George the Third's managerial indignities. Before long, he began thinking that if Uncle Tom were to come back on deck and announce they were changing course for Africa, he would not have resisted. At this moment in time, nothing appealed to him more than the thought of sailing the ocean blue with Alicia Farrell at this side.

By noontime, the Happy Ending was well underway, making ten knots. Lunch in the cockpit consisted of fried chicken from a cardboard bucket Mary passed among the four of them, and mugs of hot coffee to lessen the chill of the ocean breezes. Much cooler than in the morning, the weather was bright and blustery. Gibb had stowed his slicker in favor of his foul weather parka. The other crewmembers had changed into warmer gear—jump suits with elastic inner cuffs sealing off their wrists, and rubber boots to keep their feet dry. Their spirits could not have been higher.

By mid-afternoon, they were well clear of Long Island Sound, tacking and jibing in the open ocean. Gibb was alone at the helm when the vessel encountered a series of long rolling swells rising and falling under the bow. To the northeast, a steep pile of black cumulonimbus clouds appeared, overlaying a thick swirl of dark grey, ominous appearing, flat bases. On the bulkhead, the barometer was plunging. Gibb was experienced enough to recognize the danger signals. An ugly squall line was rapidly forming, signaling the onslaught of gale force winds and heavy seas.

Gibb was wondering whether the four of them were crew enough to ride out the rapidly approaching storm when, without warning, Uncle Tom came charging up the companionway. He was wearing a large-brimmed sou'wester tightly tied under his chin. In his right hand, he clutched a copy of the latest weatherfax. Pointing towards the squall line, he shouted at Gibb in the command voice.

"I'm afraid we're in for a bad one."

Gibb was holding the wheel steady on a northeasterly course.

"Should I bring her about and head for port?"

Uncle Tom's look was as grim as any Gibb had ever encountered during the summer he crewed on the Perkins' schooner.

"It's safer to hold course and heave-to," Uncle Tom said in a gruff voice.

Gibb hove-to. It was then that their luck went bad. Those dark grey clouds turned black at the water-line, bringing driving rain ahead of the heavy winds. Thunder and massive bolts of lightening in shifting patterns accompanied the rain, churning the seas and rocking the boat. Waves of increasing size began breaking over the bow. The waves sprayed the cockpit. They raised Gibb's anxiety level several notches.

"All hands on deck!" Uncle Tom shouted down the companionway.

"Aye, aye, skipper!" Mary shouted back.

Again Uncle Tom shouted down the companionway, this time with even greater urgency.

"Bring up the life jackets and the safety harnesses—on the double!"

Uncle Tom relieved Gibb at the wheel. He spoke to Gibb in an anxious voice.

"I'll need you to help Alicia douse the staysail and the Yankee and double-reef the mainsail."

Uncle Tom struggled with the wheel. The wind was approaching gale force. Massive bolts of lightening had him and Gibb fearing for their lives. Ten-foot high waves battered the hull, causing the vessel to shudder.

Mary and Alicia arrived on deck outfitted for the storm. They passed out life jackets and safety harnesses to Uncle Tom and Gibb. Throwing open the port locker, Mary retrieved a pile of six-foot double tethers with stainless steel snap hooks attached. She instructed Gibb and Alicia to attach them to their safety harnesses.

Praying the snap hooks were strong enough to keep him and Alicia from being washed overboard, Gibb stepped gingerly out onto the port side-deck and lunged for the top wire of the stainless steel double life-lines. He gripped the top lifeline with both hands and inched along sideways until he was opposite the port grab rail. Inhaling deeply, he let go of the lifeline and dove for the grab rail. Alicia followed close behind him, mimicking his every move. After hooking his tether to the jack wire, he reached for Alicia's tether and hooked it to the jack wire alongside his. They held fast to the grab rail while a wave washed over them, pinning them to the cabin top.

Getting to the mast proved to be a major accomplishment. They arrived just as Uncle Tom turned the vessel head-to-wind, fluttering the sails. A series of fifteen-foot waves cascaded over them. Gibb waited for the waves to pass, before switching Alicia's tether to the mainsail halyard. Alicia held tight to the mast. She waited while Gibb switched his tether to the leeward jack wire. Afterwards, Gibb signaled for Alicia to release the halyard with the staysail winch and douse the staysail. Alicia hastily doused and secured the staysail. No sooner was the staysail secured, than she doused the Yankee.

The wildly flapping Yankee plummeted to the deck. Its top half billowed out over the starboard lifelines. Convinced it was about to blow overboard, Gibb threw himself face down upon the Yankee. He succeeded in wrestling the Yankee to the side-deck and with the sheets began lashing it to the lifelines. Working his way aft, he was able to secure all but the leech end. Before he could secure the leech end, a huge wave knocked him to his knees, heeling the vessel over on an angle and setting the starboard side-deck awash.

Gibb ended up on his back with his tether intact. He looked up at Alicia. Alicia was clinging to the mast for dear life. She had tightened her tether until she and the mast were as one. Gibb sat upright and braced himself against the bulkhead. A second wave exploded in Alicia's face with enough force to tear her snap hook loose from the halyard. A torrent of water propelled her headlong towards the place on the side-deck where

Gibb was sitting. They were now in the midst of a full-fledged gale, bringing with it Force 10 winds. Gibb was terrified. Never in his life had he been this afraid. Not even when engaged in his worst street fights—the ones where he was forced to defend himself against more than one gangbanger at the same time.

Alicia's midsection thudded against the lifelines a few feet from Gibb. In desperation, Gibb reached out as if through a waterfall and caught Alicia by the legs, saving her from being washed overboard. He dragged her alongside him, rolled her over on her stomach, and lay face down on top of her, shielding her from a third booming wave. After the third wave passed, Alicia began vomiting seawater and groaning loudly enough for Gibb to hear her over the sound of the howling wind.

In a state of alarm, Gibb told himself to focus on getting Alicia back to the cockpit without either of them being washed overboard. Doubting this was possible without the aid of his tether, he chanced leaving Alicia on the side-deck while he unhooked his tether from the leeward jack wire and fastened it to the one running alongside the starboard grab rail. This maneuver freed him to wrap the tether around Alicia's waist and to hook it to her harness ring. Bound together by the tether, and with his left hand gripping the grab rail and his right arm extended across Alicia's chest and under her armpit, he dragged her limp body backwards along the side-deck.

When at last they were alongside the cockpit, Mary was waiting there to help haul Alicia onto the deck. Gibb unhooked his tether from the jack wire and climbed into the cockpit behind Alicia. Mary opened the hatch.

She helped Gibb lower Alicia below deck. Struggling to maintain their footing, they maneuvered Alicia's body down the passageway and lifted her onto her berth in the forward cabin opposite the one assigned to Gibb.

The vessel's constant rolling reminded Gibb of the dangerous conditions on deck. Leaving Mary to attend to Alicia, he made his way aft to the companion-way ladder. He scrambled back up the ladder into the cockpit and battened down the cockpit hatch. Uncle Tom was hard at work lashing the helm all the way to the leeward, in the hove-to position. With the wheel secured, he pointed Gibb towards the heaving port side-deck and into the face of a fifty-mile an hour wind.

"If we don't double reef the mainsail in a hurry," Uncle Tom shouted into the wind, "we're liable to capsize. Go forward and use the mainsail winch to drop the mainsail. We'll need to reef from both ends."

Gingerly skirting the cockpit dodger, Gibb dove for the port grab rail. Behind him, Uncle Tom slipped under the boom and steadied himself on the cabin top. With both hands, he held on tight to the top of the traveler. Gibb worked his way along the grab rail to the base of the mast. Climbing onto the cabin top, he shortened his tether and succeeded in tightening the topping lift before being driven to his knees by another huge wave.

Gibb had only reefed a sail once. This time, he prayed for divine guidance. He knew the trick was to release the mainsail halyard just enough so that the luff cringle—the eyelet used to connect the furled mainsail to the boom—was positioned for a double reef, and no further. But he couldn't get the mainsail winch to cooperate. Each time he attempted to turn the handle, the winch jammed.

Hard as he tried, Gibb could not free the winch. He had given up hope when Uncle Tom appeared alongside him. Uncle Tom grabbed for the mainsail halyard and yanked on it. Gibb braced himself against the bulkhead. With all his strength, he pushed down on the winch handle one last time. His prayers were answered when the winch gave way and the mainsail came tumbling down. Seizing the luff with both hands, he pulled hard on the flapping sail until he was able to secure it to the tack hook at the point where the boom was fastened to the mast.

While Gibb was attending to the luff cringle, Uncle Tom slid around him and worked his way aft along the boom. He succeeded in reaching the traveler. But before he could tension the luff cringle's counterpart, he was felled by an enormous wave. The wave sent him tumbling backwards. Gibb was horrified, watching the force of the wave drive Uncle Tom's body head first into a lifeline stanchion and then out of sight. The free end of the mainsail was flapping wildly and in danger of being ripped to pieces. Gibb went aft in search of Uncle Tom's body. Dropping down onto the heaving port sidedeck, he found Uncle Tom lying face down opposite the cockpit dodger. All the while, wind and rain and rollicking waves were punishing the Happy Ending to such a degree, the vessel was in imminent danger of going down with all hands aboard.

Gibb dropped to his knees and turned Uncle Tom over on his back. Although unconscious, Uncle Tom was alive and breathing, unburdening Gibb of his worst fears. Blood was streaming down Uncle Tom's face from a large gash in his forehead. It took all of Gibb's strength to drag Uncle Tom's limp body backwards into the cockpit, where he lay stretched out on the deck, unconscious. Gibb knelt over Uncle Tom, slapping him lightly on both cheeks, seeking to revive him. Several slaps later, Uncle Tom came to, coughing up seawater. Grasping Gibb's neck with both hands, he pulled Gibb's head down towards him.

"Reefing won't be enough to save this ship," he said in a weakened voice. "We'll have to deploy the drogue and try running on bare poles."

"Wouldn't that be risky?"

Uncle Tom struggled to sit up.

"Under these conditions, anything we try is risky. Either we cut our speed in half in a hurry, or she'll break apart. Go back and douse the mainsail when I bring her head-to-wind."

Gibb scrambled forward to release the mainsail halyard. The mainsail plummeted to the cabin top. Gibb worked his way back to the cockpit, lashing the mainsail to the boom as he went along. Uncle Tom was at the wheel and back in command. The bandana he had tied around his forehead had stopped the bleeding. All he needed was a gold earring, thought Gibb, and he could have passed for a pirate on the run.

"Go below and get the drogue from Mary," said Uncle Tom. "And be quick about it."

Gibb threw open the cockpit hatch. He dropped down the companionway ladder. Mary was sprawled on the galley deck surrounded by objects the storm had broken loose. Her complexion was a shade of green. She stared at him blankly.

"We need the drogue in a hurry," said Gibb.

Using both of her hands, Mary grabbed hold of the sink and pulled herself to her feet. The drogue was stored in an aft compartment among tanks of stove gas and lanterns and cordage and an assortment of marine hardware. Mary pulled loose the cone-shaped drogue with its 200 feet of nylon anchor rode. She passed it back to Gibb. Gibb dragged the drogue to the companionway. He heaved it up to the cockpit and climbed back on deck.

"Lead the bitter end of the rode through the starboard chock and secure it around the coffee grinder," Uncle Tom shouted into the Force 10 winds in the voice of a Navy commander.

Gibb followed Uncle Tom's instructions to the letter. Once he had secured the line, he paid the rode out into the churning sea until all but a few feet were submerged. Carefully he lowered the drogue over the side and watched it sink.

Gibb turned to face Uncle Tom.

"What happens now?"

"We should feel the shock when the drogue fetches up at the end of the rode." Uncle Tom paused. "Can't say for sure—'cause this is the first time I ever had to deploy one."

Gibb experienced another moment of panic. Fearing the drogue would fail them, he leaned over the stern and watched, wondering whether they would have to abandon ship. He needn't have worried. The drogue soon took hold and the vessel began to shudder. A few minutes later, the vessel's speed was cut in half. Gibb turned to face Uncle Tom. Uncle Tom pointed towards the horizon.

"From the looks of things, it won't be long before she blows herself out," he said in a reassuring voice. "You'd better go below and check on Alicia—this experience isn't going to make it any easier for her to make up her mind."

"About what?"

"About marrying that arrogant son of a bitch, Josh Bingham."

Gibb threw the skipper a half-hearted salute, before lowering himself down the companionway ladder. Mary was standing in the galley brewing tea. The color had returned to her cheeks. Gibb undid his life jacket and his parka and tossed them on the chart table. He asked Mary how Alicia was? Mary said Alicia was a lot tougher than she looked.

Gibb sat on the galley deck. He propped himself up, his back resting against the bulkhead. Mary passed him a mug of hot tea. He sipped the tea and savored the warm sensation in his throat. Mary smiled at him in the manner of a person who was now a comrade-in-arms. Gibb looked up at her.

"What does Uncle Tom have against Josh Jr.?" he asked, wondering whether unknowingly he had been enlisted in a conspiracy.

"He thinks Josh Jr. is a stuffed shirt."

"Wouldn't that be a little like the pot calling the kettle black?"

"Being a stuffed shirt is one thing—being an arrogant stuffed shirt is another. And it doesn't help that Josh Jr. would much rather row than sail."

Gibb finished his tea. He said to himself it was time to check on Alicia. When making his way down the passageway to Alicia's cabin, his mind began to wander. The thought came to him about Alicia having lured him on board—and then about how close he came to losing her to the stormy seas—and about the comments Uncle Tom and Mary made about Josh Bingham—and about Sally being in the hospital. In his weakened condition, he had difficulty putting the pieces of this puzzle together.

When he reached Alicia's cabin, the door was open a crack. Alicia was lying in her berth, halfway under the covers. Gibb assumed she was asleep. Gently, he closed the door and stepped back from it.

Alicia called out to him.

"I'm awake—whoever you are."

Gibb pushed open the door and hesitantly stepped inside.

"I was hoping it was you," said Alicia in a subdued voice. "Come closer—there's something I have to tell you—and I don't want anyone else to hear me."

Gibb moved to Alicia's side. She patted the bunk, motioning for him to sit down beside her. He sat on the edge of the bunk and leaned towards her. She reached up and, bringing his head close to her lips, she whispered in his ear.

"I owe you my life."

Gibb was flustered. Gently as he was able, he moved back away from her. She smiled at his discomfort. Embarrassed and more confused than ever about her intentions, he got to his feet and abruptly backed away towards the cabin door.

"There's nothing for you to worry about," said he in a reassuring voice. "I promise you—I'll never try to collect."

"You really know how to disappoint a woman."

Again Gibb was flustered.

"I'd better relieve Uncle Tom at the wheel," he said in a hoarse voice.

Alicia saluted him.

"Aye, aye, sir!" said she, laughingly.

Chapter

12

I n the red and gold glow of the warm late afternoon
sun, Barrows Landing was the prettiest sight Gibb
had seen in years. The howling winds and heavy seas
had been left far behind the tip of Long Island where
this sailing town was located. In their place, a gentle
offshore breeze was blowing. Seated on deckchairs in
the cockpit, Gibb and Mary were watching Uncle Tom
pilot the Happy Ending through a narrow channel
marked by buoys, leading to the inner harbor. Her flags
unfurled, the Happy Ending chugged along under
power. A fleet of sailing yachts dominated the crescent
shaped inner harbor marina. Against the backdrop of
a village waterfront lined with shops and commercial
establishments catering to the maritime trade, an

abundance of bare masts bobbed at anchor. To the north, leading away from the waterfront, church spires reached skyward, giving this port the appearance of a safe harbor from the stormiest of seas.

The marina docking area was located at mid-point on the main street. Divided into two sections, it had berths enough for two dozen good-sized vessels. Calls from greeters aboard sailing yachts and power boats riding at anchor, their glasses raised in salute, signaled to the crew of the Happy Ending that the cocktail hour was underway.

Uncle Tom turned off the engine, allowing the Happy Ending to glide towards its assigned berth. When the Happy Ending arrived alongside the dock, he ordered the fenders attached and the bow and stern lines secured. Gibb and Mary hastily complied. Alicia watched the activity from the cockpit. She was casually dressed in a denim shirt and white pants and white and blue deck shoes. Mary attached the bumpers. Gibb jumped overboard onto the dock where he secured the bow line and the stern line to cleats and waited for the others to join him.

"Drinks and dinner are on me at Shipwreck Kelly's," said Uncle Tom after his commands were fully executed.

Shipwreck Kelly's was a waterfront bar and restaurant situated on the main street a short distance from the entrance to the dock area. Wedged between a bait shop and a shop that rented bicycles, its exterior walls were covered with weathered, unpainted shingles. In the center of the roof, a weather vane was pointing in an easterly direction.

The inside of the building was a lot more colorful than the outside. To the right of the entrance, a long oak bar backed by the usual assortment of liquor bottles was packed with patrons. Above the liquor bottles, an ancient masthead extended outward from the wall a few feet below the ceiling. Unlike the ceiling in the dining area, the bar ceiling was standard in height. Casually dressed older patrons were seated on a long line of bar stools, engaged in noisy, animated conversation.

On the side of the entrance opposite the bar, dining area walls made of wide, unpainted barn wood, looking like the planks were a century or more old, reached skyward towards a cathedral ceiling. Thick overhead beams intersected in the center of the room. The beams were festooned with fishnets and lobster traps. Amber and green and red running lights were lit and evenly spaced along the walls. In keeping with the nautical theme, between the running lights, large size prints of clipper ships were encased in glass. The floor was made of pegged wood. It was covered with captain's chairs and bare wooden tables, all of them painted in black. At the far end of the dining area, next to a massive stone fireplace, a boisterous younger crowd was gathered around a grand piano singing along with the piano player to show tunes from Broadway musicals.

After ushering his crew into the bar area, Uncle Tom positioned himself between the brass rails of the service bar. From a grey-bearded old salt, he ordered drinks for his crew. The old salt wore a gold earring in each of his pierced ear lobes. He was pouring drinks at a furious pace for the lively cocktail crowd. The crew members stood nearby, waiting to be served their drinks, discussing the day's adventure.

"Heard there was one hell of a blow out there this afternoon," said the old salt to Uncle Tom.

"Nothing we couldn't handle," said Uncle Tom, proudly pointing out the members of his crew.

Gibb became distracted by a familiar voice escaping from the crowd around the piano. He turned and scanned the far end of the room. The next thing he knew, Heather Atwood and Piper Wilcox were marching towards him, drinks in hand, waving furiously. Heather was dressed in high waist, wide leg, white linen pants and a black and white T-top, Piper in skintight jeans and a designer T-shirt, showing off her nipples.

"Gibb Quinn!" Heather and Piper shouted in unison over the din.

Gibb glanced in Alicia's direction. As yet unaware of what was happening, Alicia was reaching out to Uncle Tom for a glass of white wine for herself and a bottle of beer for Gibb. She took the drinks from Uncle Tom and handed Gibb the bottle of beer. Gibb barely had time to take his first sip before Heather and Piper arrived, positioning themselves on either side of him. Unsure of whether or not Alicia had heard them calling to him, he decided his best option was to remain silent.

The conversation turned into a clash of boarding school accents.

"Haven't seen you in ages," said Piper to Alicia.

"What are you doing here?" Alicia asked.

"My friend Heather and I are spending the weekend on her date's yacht."

"Where did you meet Gibb?"

"It's a long story," said Piper.

Gibb looked down and scuffed his feet. Uncle Tom and Mary smiled at his discomfort. Alicia directed a suspicious look at Gibb.

"I imagine so," said Alicia, sarcastically.

"Someone told me Josh is spending the summer in San Francisco," said Piper, looking directly at Gibb.

"If it's of any interest to you, he's clerking at Bryce and Morehead."

"It must be very lonely for you," said Piper, returning Alicia's sarcasm.

"Not when I have someone like Gibb to play with," said Alicia, glancing at Gibb.

Gibb's face turned red and his stomach started churning. Piper seemed amused at his discomfit. She placed an arm around his waist, momentarily hugging him tight. Gibb glanced sideways at her. Her erect nipples looked to him as though they were about to burst through her designer T-shirt.

"I'm still waiting for that invitation to Chatham," she said to Gibb in a stage whisper.

Uncle Tom stepped between Gibb and Piper, splitting them apart.

"Don't Mary and I rate an introduction?" he asked Piper.

Before Piper could answer him, the remainder of the crowd from around the piano descended upon the group, laughing and joking and mixing people together. A lot of animated cocktail talk followed. Drinks were reordered. People switched places back and forth, discussing the storm the Happy Ending had encountered and ocean racing and the price of rentals in the

Hamptons and the two-pound Maine lobsters featured on Shipwreck Kelly's dinner menu. Throughout the cocktail hour, Piper flirted openly with Gibb. The more uncomfortable he became, the harder Piper pressed him for an invitation to Chatham.

When the cocktail hour ended, the two groups dined at tables close to one another. For the Happy Ending's crew, dinner was a subdued affair made more solemn by Alicia's irritability at Piper Wilcox. With words and gestures, Piper continued to flirt with Gibb the entire time. Uncle Tom did his best to distract Alicia by revisiting and making light of the afternoon's stormy ordeal. Gibb wondered why Alicia was acting territorially. As far as he knew, her fight with Josh Jr. had not changed her mind about marrying him. *Why else,* he asked himself, *would she still be wearing her 4-carat diamond engagement ring?* He supposed Piper was asking herself the same question.

Uncle Tom had just finished declaring that, but for Gibb's seamanship, the Happy Ending would be resting in Davy Jones's Locker, when Piper and her group passed by the table on their way to the exit. Piper paused behind Gibb. She brushed her cheek against his. Alicia looked on in stony silence.

"Call me," said Piper in a stage whisper.

Half and hour later, Uncle Tom called for the check. When the waitress brought the check, he announced that he and Mary intended to repair to the bar for an after dinner drink and that Gibb and Alicia were welcome to join them. Gibb glanced at Alicia for direction. Alicia shook her head from side to side. Her arms were folded and her jaw was taut. Gibb shrugged his shoulders, signaling that the choice was hers to make.

Shortly thereafter, Alicia left Shipwreck Kelly's ahead of Gibb. As she marched in silence down the pier towards the Happy Ending's berth, she spied an empty soft drink can sitting upright in the middle of the pier. Making a run at the soft drink can, she kicked it high and long. Just as the can took flight, Gibb caught up with her.

"Something bothering you?"

"I'm sure she could make lots of money in a place like Las Vegas," said Alicia, sarcastically.

"Are you talking about Piper Wilcox?"

"You know damn well who I'm talking about! She who kept rubbing her big boobs against your chest— she who in her senior year at Harvard had a reputation for snorting coke and giving nude dinner parties."

"That's a pretty mean thing to say about anybody."

"I knew you were a streets guy. But I never figured you for being one of those nipple nuts."

"And I never figured you for being a placekicker. Does that make us even?"

With a wave of her hand, Alicia brushed off Gibb's last question.

"I'm still waiting for that invitation to Chatham," said she, mimicking Piper Wilcox's deep voice and mannerisms.

"Why would someone who's engaged care one way or another?"

"It's not a girl-guy thing," said Alicia in earnest. "If that's what you're thinking."

"I'll bite—what kind of a thing is it?"

"A competitive thing."

Gibb placed a hand on Alicia's shoulder.

"Believe me," said he sympathetically. "That kind of thing I understand perfectly."

A short time later, Alicia was seated on the forward deck of the Happy Ending with her back against the hatch. Her arms were locked around her knees. She was looking up at the moon and stars. Gibb approached her from the starboard side-deck, bearing a glass of savignon blanc and a bottle of beer. He handed the glass of wine to Alicia and sat down beside her. He was surprised to see that she was not wearing her engagement ring. The wind had died down completely and the surface of the water was perfectly calm.

"I apologize for the way I acted tonight Your relationship with Piper is none of my business."

"I wouldn't characterize a one night stand as a relationship."

"I'm a lot more interested in hearing about your father."

Gibb fell silent. He was leery of allowing Alicia inside his defense perimeter. Alicia seemed to sense what was on his mind.

"You can trust me," said she in a quiet, reassuring voice. "I swear to you, I'll never say a word about it to anyone."

Gibb stared at Alicia, wondering what would happen if he turned her down, even though she promised to be discreet. *"What the hell!"*—he said to himself after a long pause.

"The guy was a real bum," said Gibb, matter-of-factly. "I'll never forgive him for the way he treated my mother."

"What did he do for a living?"

"As far as I knew—when I was growing up—mostly he gambled. He loved the action. Whenever he had money, he'd rent a room on the Strip and hang out with high priced hookers and gangsters, shooting craps."

Alicia took Gibb's free hand in hers.

"Did he ever live with you?"

"Only when he was down on his luck. He'd come barging into the trailer, slapping my mother around until she gave him all the money she'd saved. The next day, off he'd go again."

"He doesn't sound like the type who had much to teach a son."

"I don't know—he taught me how to cheat at cards—and how to tell real gold chains from fake ones—and he always knew which white loafers were the best buy."

Alicia stood and pulled Gibb to his feet. She took his beer bottle from him and placed it on the hatch alongside her wine glass.

"I'm being serious."

Gibb sought to foreclose on this subject.

"As far as I'm concerned, I'm an orphan."

"Do you know what became of him?"

"Word around Vegas was, he won a McDonald's restaurant franchise in a high stakes poker game and parlayed it into a chain of them. Last I heard he and his child bride were living in a big house in Fresno—driving Lexuses and sending their kids to private schools. Not bad for a bum from *the war zone.*"

"When was the last time you saw him?"

"Can't remember that far back."

Alicia took Gibb by the hand and led him into the pulpit. They leaned against the railing, gazing up at the moon.

"I've got a cure for your *war zone* blues."

"What kind of a cure?"

Alicia placed her arms around Gibb's neck and drew his head towards hers. They were interrupted by noises coming from the cockpit.

"Captain coming aboard!" said Uncle Tom in a loud voice.

Alicia drew away from Gibb.

"Thanks a lot, Uncle Tom," said she in a voice so low, Gibb had trouble hearing her.

✿ ✿ ✿

Early on Sunday morning, Alicia slipped into Gibb's cabin, awakening him out of a sound sleep. Pressing a finger to her lips, she beckoned for him to get dressed and meet her in the cockpit. Gibb pulled back the covers. He staggered out from under his double berth and pulled on his khakis. Still half asleep, he tiptoed over to a cramped head. The head smelled of Alicia's perfume. Except for the sound of the refrigerator door opening and closing, all was quiet below the top deck. Gibb washed and shaved hurriedly, before joining Alicia in the cockpit.

Alicia handed him a large glass of orange juice. To the east, the sun was barely rising over the horizon. In the dock area, all was quiet aboard the rows of sailing

yachts and power boats. Out in the harbor, sport fishermen proceeded in single file, heading for the channel.
The sound of their diesel engines was the only noise
breaking the early morning silence. Waves from their
wakes gently rocked the Happy Ending. High above,
gulls were circling, then pealing off to dive for prey. Not
a sole was stirring on the waterfront.

"What's up?" Gibb asked Alicia in a low voice.

"We're going for a walk," said Alicia, climbing over
the lifelines onto the dock.

Gibb deposited his empty juice glass on the starboard locker. He followed Alicia over the side. They
walked the length of the pier in silence, then continued past Shipwreck Kelly's all the way to the north end
of main street. A turnoff led them to the doorstep of
Saint Anthony's Catholic church. The church was a
small wood-framed building. Its stained glass windows
stood out against the plain white exterior. Other early
risers were trickling inside for the six o'clock Mass. All
of them were casually dressed and talking in whispers,
seemingly there to attend a funeral. Desperate Gibb
was for any excuse that would allow him to avoid going
inside. Suddenly, as if prompted by divine intervention,
his reluctance gave way to the memory of his previous
day's series of heavenly entreaties. He figured this was
reason enough for him to allow Alicia to shepherd him
inside.

They settled into a middle pew and waited in silence
for the priest to appear. The elderly priest entered
from the sacristy, followed by a young acolyte. It was an
effort for Gibb to remain in his seat until the liturgy
ended. Thoughts of his mother streamed through his

consciousness, as he feared they would. He pictured her closed coffin resting in front of the altar at the Guardian Angel Cathedral on Desert Inn Road, just off *the Strip*. The Guardian Angel Cathedral wasn't their parish. It happened to be his mother's favorite place to attend Mass. He was just as angry as he was that day years before over the fact that only three other persons came to pay their respects. All three were housekeepers from the downtown casino where she had worked last. He knew of other housekeepers and a few neighbors who should have been there, but couldn't be bothered. He was even angrier at God for not allowing his mother to live long enough for him to move her out of the trailer park to an apartment in a decent neighborhood. The fact that God had spared him from the storm at sea was not enough to change his attitude. He was not ready to forgive God—not now—maybe not ever.

"The Mass has ended, go in peace to love and serve the Lord," said the priest, at last.

"You were thinking about your mother the whole time, weren't you?" Alicia whispered to Gibb on their way outside.

"How could you tell?"

Alicia took him by the arm.

"I'm getting better at reading your mind."

Chapter

13

Word of Gibb's weekend sail ricocheted around Chatham Township at a speed and intensity impressing even the most experienced gossipmongers. The Chatham rumor mill functioned much like the party line telephone systems of yesteryear. Art Donovan was the first to pass the rumor along to Gibb. Art heard it from the manager of Bingham's Hardware, or so Art claimed. The manager of Bingham's Hardware heard it from the high school custodian—who'd heard it from the chief mechanic at the garage on Water Street. The chief mechanic had heard it from a customer with a big mouth that claimed to have spotted Gibb and Alicia leaving the Yacht Club parking lot on Sunday afternoon in her BMW convertible. The rumor was confirmed by a member of the Chatham Yacht Club. He claimed to have seen Alicia and Gibb holding hands coming out of the Catholic Church at Barrrows Landing, acting like lovers. The latter intelligence report was all the proof the Regulars needed to convict Gibb of a crime of passion. It mattered not to any of these God-fearing Christians that gossip was the devil's radio.

According to what Art told Gibb during his urgent Monday afternoon telephone alert, the Regulars were demanding to know how Judge Farrell's daughter could spend the money to fly all the way to San Francisco to be with her fiancé and then have the nerve to come home and go for a weekend sail with a cowboy from Las Vegas? This was more than the Regulars could bear. Worse yet, the entire membership of the Chatham Beach Improvement Society was vowing never to rest until the Vegas cowboy was forced to leave them and their town alone.

Was he witnessing the start of the Apocalypse, Gibb was wondering when Gerry charged into his office and plunked herself down on his spare chair. She was laughing at the stories being passed from store to store along Main Street before coming to rest at the Big Byte checkout counter. Never in her memory had any communiqué travelled this fast since the widowed choirmaster at the Methodist church turned up pregnant at Christmastime five years before.

Gibb was more worried than he had been during the entire ordeal at sea. Overcome by a feeling of impending doom, he rubbed his eyes and with a scowl on his face only half-listened to Gerry.

"You'll either have to propose to her or prepare to defend yourself," Gerry said in a humorous manner.

"Whichever way you choose, they'll end up lynching you or running you out of town on a rail."

"The good news is they can only kill me once. Now tell me more about the foil?"

"I presume you're referring to Mary Walsh. She grew up in a run-down neighborhood in New Haven. Comes from a family of eight kids. Her father was a trash hauler for the Department of Public Works. He died of lung cancer two years ago. From what I've heard from Art Donovan, her family had a lot to overcome."

"She seemed pretty stable to me."

"Her being Tom Farrell's mistress drives Judge Farrell crazy. And you'll end up in the same boat, if you don't leave Alicia alone."

"How many times do I have to tell you, Alicia and I are just good friends."

"That's what Mary Walsh tells people about Tom Farrell."

"I don't suppose it's any of their business. Is it?"

"They say she had an abortion. True or not, the sad thing is she might as well leave town. The Farrells will never accept her."

They were interrupted by a telephone call from Alicia. She was calling to invite Gibb to dinner with her parents on Saturday evening. Gibb was so non-plussed, he repeated the latest rumor verbatim. Alicia was livid. Her response was loud enough for Gerry to overhear. She sputtered and stammered, declaring it was time people in this town understood that a person did not have to graduate from Yale in order to qualify as a friend of hers. Gibb interrupted her tirade in order to tell Alicia he was accepting her invitation. Their conversation ended abruptly.

He ran his fingers through his hair. The feeling of impending doom returned. A look of deep concern clouded his face.

"This could be the kiss of death for our local sales."

"What's the difference?" Gerry asked. "The whole town's convinced you and Alicia are having an affair?"

"Any news from Sister Mary Elizabeth?" Gibb asked, leaning back in his chair with his hands behind his head, seeking to change the subject.

"I was waiting until closing time to give you the bad news. Over the weekend, she was transferred to the state hospital in Middletown."

Gibb banged a fist on the top of his desk.

"She could have made it—if only she was willing to try."

"She gave up a long time ago Gibb. Short of marrying her, there was nothing you could do to save her."

✿ ✿ ✿

At eight o'clock Saturday afternoon, Gibb was behind the wheel of his rental car, dodging the tourists on Main Street. Ahead of him, on the town green, people were gathered around the Victorian bandstand, licking their ice cream cones, waiting for the evening band concert to begin. He glided past, turning right at the Methodist Church where the road branched off towards a series of wooded estates. A mile further along, he turned into the driveway to the Farrell mansion and drove around back to the three-car garage. He parked the car in front of the garage, in the rearview mirror checking to make sure every hair was in place. Nattily attired in a tan summer suit, striped shirt and silk tie and tasseled loafers, he followed the flagstone walkway around to the front entrance. He was hoping against hope that his wardrobe selection would provide a shield against the type of inquisition he dreaded. Little did he realize that the better dressed he was judged to be, the more certain Alicia's parents would view him as a serious threat to their daughter's future well-being.

Beds of impatiens in red, white and pink, flanked the flagstone sidewalk. Alongside him, carefully tended shrubbery was rimmed by colorful displays of poppies and Black-eyed Susans and day lilies. Rows of lilac bushes separated the driveway from a high stone wall reaching all the way to the back of the main house. Behind the stone wall the tops of an imposing stand of oak trees were visible. There appeared to be a much larger expanse of front lawn than Gibb remembered from his Christmas Eve visit. The main house, however, was exactly as he remembered it—very large and graceful and white and green and beautiful. All of the windows on the ground floor were screened and open. To Gibb the condition of the property signified that the owners were people of boundless wealth. *Old money* was the expression he recalled the Regulars most often prefacing their remarks with when discussing the people who resided in this section of town.

Alicia was waiting for him at the front door. She was wearing her 4-carat diamond engagement ring. Gibb stepped inside. He greeted her with a polite handshake. She was dressed in a lavender silk blouse and a white ankle-length linen skirt and sandals, and she looked lovely. During their passage past the spacious front staircase and down the hall corridor to a set of French doors at the rear of the house, Gibb decided that the best way for him to survive the evening would be to speak only when spoken to. The French doors opened out to a large screened porch furnished in white wicker. Big baskets of mums graced the porch at strategic locations, contrasting nicely with the white wicker furniture and the white brick walls lined with Bengert floral prints.

Judge Farrell stood at a side table mixing martinis. He was dressed in a navy blue blazer and white pants, looking very much like a Yale alumnus from the Class of 1973. In front of him, bottles of expensive liquor were arranged on a sterling silver tray. On an adjoining sterling silver tray, surrounded by an assortment of crystal glasses, an open bottle of sauvignon blanc from a Napa Valley winery was cooling in a sterling silver ice bucket. Nearby stood Alicia's mother in her long summer dress, beautifully coifed and smiling at Gibb. The parents greeted Gibb with formal handshakes, cool and correct, as if intending to set the tone for the evening.

Gibb stared past the parents at the swimming pool and tennis court in the terraced area behind the house. He was thinking that he felt more relaxed when in the presence of George the Third. After declining Judge Farrell's offer of a martini, he thought better of asking for a bottle of beer, opting instead for a glass of wine. Judge Farrell poured him and Alicia each a glass of savignon blanc and handed the glasses to them.

"I'm told this is what my brother Tom serves aboard the Happy Ending," said the judge to Gibb with the accusatory look of a skeptical jurist.

Alicia took Gibb by the arm and steered him out of the line of fire.

"Right you are, father," said she in a manner, suggesting to her father that the subject of the weekend she and Gibb spent on her uncle's yacht was off limits.

Judge Farrell obliged Alicia by launching into a tirade about the prolifigate spending habits of the Democrats in Congress having caused the current trillion dollar deficits and having brought the country to the brink of ruin. Politically speaking, ever since he became old enough to vote, Gibb had been an Independent. He assumed there was enough blame on both sides of the political isle to keep anyone, including Judge Farrell, from pinning the blame on one party or the other for the financial mess the country was in. For this reason, he thought it best to remain silent while the judge rambled on about the liberals in Congress and their socialist ideas being the root cause of all of the country's problems, be they domestic or foreign.

At strategic intervals, Alicia raised her eyebrows, signaling to Gibb that she did not share her father's very conservative views. This was enough to pacify Gibb. Not being the first time Gibb had been confronted with arguments like these, he braced himself for the predictable assault on the Senate Majority Leader. Judge Farrell did not disappoint him.

"It's all because of your Senator Harry Reid," the judge said at last, his face becoming redder by the minute. "That socialist should be impeached. He's out to destroy this country."

"Senator Reid is a member of the Mormon Church," said Gibb. "As far as I know, there aren't any Mormon socialists."

Alicia smiled and sipped her wine.

"He certainly acts like a socialist," said the judge.

"I don't know much about politics, but from personal experience I do know that Senator Reid really cares about people. If it wasn't for him, my mother wouldn't have lived long enough to see me graduate from college."

"Would you mind explaining what that's supposed to mean?"

"My mother worked for one of the nonunion hotels in Las Vegas and she didn't have any health insurance. When she found out she had cancer, Senator Reid is the one who made the call that got her into a free treatment program."

"After watching him on television, no doubt he did it to get your mother's vote."

"Father!" said a visibly upset Alicia, raising her voice precipitously.

Gibb's stomach was churning. He was tempted to punch the judge in the face. It was then that his survival instincts took control of him. Reminding himself of what a mistake it would be to alienate the man whose wife was the source of so many Big Byte referrals, he put down his wine glass and asked Alicia to direct him to the nearest john. Alicia took him by the arm and pointed him in the direction of the hallway.

"By the way," said Gibb over his shoulder when he was halfway out of the room. "In Las Vegas, dead people aren't allowed to vote."

The rest of the cocktail hour passed without any further discussion of Washington politics and without any mention of Josh Jr. or of the contentious weekend sail. Gibb was thankful when one of the uniformed maids announced that dinner was served. They entered the dining room single file through double doors off of the front hallway. Gibb was overwhelmed by the appearance of colonial splendor this high-ceilinged replica of the Federal period presented. Only in the copies of Architectural Digest lining an end table in his dentist's office in Seattle had Gibb ever before seen such an authentic replica. Done in white plaster and yellow wood paneling reaching to the chair rail, the dining room resembled a scene from the grand old houses in Virginia. Its most striking feature was a spacious fireplace built into the wall opposite the entrance. Over the fireplace, in an ornate gilded frame, hung a really large portrait of one of the colonial governors of Connecticut.

A crystal chandelier was centered above the highly polished mahogany dining room table. The table was set with linen place mats and flowers and silver candelabra and fine china and sterling silver place settings. Eight ladderback Chippendale chairs were perfectly spaced around the table, three on each side and one on each end. The table rested on a colorful Persian rug that complimented the pegged wood floor. Just below the ceiling, an ornate white cornice molding stretched along the top of the entire room. From Gibb's point of view, all that was missing were colonial attendants in white silk stockings and ruffled cuffs and powdered wigs.

If the Farrell's purpose was to intimidate Gibb, they succeeded handsomely. He turned to Mrs. Farrell for his seat assignment. She motioned for him to sit next to her on the opposite side of the table facing Alicia. The judge occupied the end chair nearest to Mrs. Farrell. No sooner were all of them seated, than the uniformed maid served them the first course—fruit compost in frosted crystal dishes with linen doilies underneath them. She also poured each of them a glass of the same white wine the judge had served to Gibb and Alicia during the cocktail hour.

The judge said grace. When the judge was finished, Mrs. Farrell turned to Gibb, as if expecting him to comment. Gibb was hoping a compliment would lighten the atmosphere.

"This is such a beautiful dining room," said he, turning to Mrs. Farrell.

"Coming from a place like Las Vegas, I should think you would find it a bit old fashioned," Judge Farrell said in response.

"Before moving to Chatham, Gibb lived in Seattle," said Alicia, defensively.

"I'm more curious about what one does growing up in a place like Las Vegas," said Judge Farrell to Gibb.

"I take it you've been there," said Gibb.

"Heavens no!"

"It's not such a bad place to grow up in."

"Assuming one is partial to gangsters and legalized prostitution and tacky neon signs and wedding chapels with drive-in windows."

Judge Farrell's last remark prompted a fit of coughing from Mrs. Farrell. Having been forewarned that the former Elisabeth Davenport was the kind of person for whom the most unpardonable sin of all was bad manners, Gibb assumed Mrs. Farrell had intended to send the judge a message that his manners were intolerable. He also assumed it would be fruitless for him to argue that the gangsters were long gone—that prostitution was legal only in Nevada's *cow counties*— and that the tackiest neon signs had been taken down and were stored in an outdoor museum on the edge of downtown Las Vegas called the Neon Boneyard Park.

Judge Farrell chose to ignore Mrs. Farrell's attempt to intervene.

"My clerk tells me you have a horrendous drug problem in Las Vegas," said he to Gibb.

"Not any worse than in Seattle."

"Or Chatham, either," said Mrs. Farrell. "From what I've been told."

"Are you back on that cocktail waitress's case again?" the judge asked Mrs. Farrell.

"You promised you'd have that hoodlum Mel Price run out of town for what he did to that poor girl."

"How many times do I have to tell you, Chief Nickerson did the best he could?"

"Obviously, it wasn't good enough. At the Garden Club they say he's back peddling cocaine to those health club clients of his."

"What was Caleb supposed to do when a greasy mob lawyer from New Haven showed up waving a copy of the Constitution in his face."

"Leaving Mel Price free to roar around town on his motorcycle, acting as if he owns this town," said Mrs. Farrell, testily

Mrs. Farrell's last remark seemed to sting the judge. Thrusting the palms of both hands towards her face, he signaled his intention to avoid any further discussion of Sally Kilgore or Mel Price.

"From what I've read, Nevada ranks at or near the bottom in almost every category," said the judge to Gibb in a superior manner.

Gibb was vaguely aware of the current statistics and of how impossible it would have been to try and defend Nevada's place in the rankings to a Connecticut snob like Judge Farrell. He reminded himself of what little success he'd ever had defending Las Vegas to people in Seattle who were a lot less judgmental. This thought caused him to punt.

"That depends on who you ask."

The judge brushed Gibb's last remark aside.

"What can you expect from a place that prides itself on being called *Sin City*," said he. "And where the mayor parades around with a martini glass in one hand, holding a half naked show girl with the other."

"No doubt about it," Gibb said with an embarrassed look on his face. "Las Vegas is a very colorful place."

"Colorful is right," said Judge Farrell. "It's hard to imagine how any city could adopt as its motto a saying as offensive as—'*What plays in Vegas stays in Vegas!*'"

Gibb assumed the judge's relentless assault on Las Vegas' image was meant as a signal to him that all was lost.

"They don't call it the entertainment capital of the world for nothing," said Gibb, facetiously.

Mrs. Farrell coughed again, this time accompanied by a warning look directed at the judge. It was obvious to Gibb that she was signaling for a truce. The judge relented and a truce ensued. The truce allowed the four of them to consume their first course in silence. As soon as they were finished with the first course—as if on cue—the maid reappeared. Clearing away the frosted crystal dishes, she replaced them with filet of baked cod cooked in a pastry shell. A few bites later, the conversation resumed.

"You are aware that Alicia is going to law school, this fall," said the judge to Gibb. "Are you not?"

"I certainly am."

"In the East, you can't get very far without a graduate degree."

"A lot of my classmates chose not to go to graduate school," said Alicia.

"That's a luxury Yale graduates can afford. It's not the same with schools no one has ever heard of."

Gibb took a sip of his wine. His face was flushed.

"Everyone can't go to Yale."

"That's the first sensible thing you've said since you returned from San Francisco."

Being criticized by her father in Gibb's presence visibly upset Alicia. Looking as though she wanted to crack a plate over his head, she excused herself to go to the powder room. The judge did not resume speaking to Gibb until Alicia was out of earshot.

"You are aware our daughter is engaged to Josh Bingham, are you not?"

Gibb wondered where this line of questioning would lead.

"I am," said he, impassively.

"It would be better for all concerned, if you would find yourself another cocktail waitress and leave our daughter alone."

Gibb's face turned beet red. Mrs. Farrell was appalled at her husband's display of bad manners. She picked at her food, in silence waiting for Alicia to return. Beads of perspiration appeared on Gibb's forehead. He was thinking that, given a choice, he would have been better off being back on the rollicking side-deck of the Happy Ending, suffering the wrath of the angry sea god Neptune.

Alicia reappeared while the maid was serving dessert. An awkward stiffness prevailed during the remainder of the meal. Alicia and her mother passed the time making light conversation about Early American antiques and other more mundane matters. Gibb and the judge were relegated to being spectators, allowing for a more peaceful interlude.

At last, Alicia declared the dinner to be at an end. She said so in a manner suggesting that this was the last time she would ever invite a guest to their dinner table. Her mother plainly was embarrassed. The judge was unmoved. His look was just as stern as it had been during the entire meal. Mrs. Farrell summoned the maid and instructed her to serve her and the judge espresso in the living room. With this accomplished, she took the judge by the arm and led him away. Alicia and Gibb remained behind, momentarily.

"I'll walk you to your car," said Alicia to Gibb. "But first I need to say goodnight to the cook."

Gibb walked alone down the main hallway to the front door. Silently and stealthily, he slipped past the entrance to the living room. The Farrells were seated opposite each other. They were engaged in a heated conversation, seemingly unconcerned whether or not they could be overheard. The conversation was loud enough for Gibb to understand every word spoken.

"Your manners were absolutely appalling tonight," said Mrs. Farrell.

"Our daughter is being pursued by a gigolo from *Sin City* and all you're worried about are my *manners*! The nerve of him trying to impress us, coming here dressed like he graduated from Choate or Hotchkiss. And this wasn't the first time. I can promise you, I wasn't fooled for one minute—not this time— and not the last time either."

"For God's sake, Buck! She owes her life to him."

"Why on earth do you suppose I was so hard on him?"

Gibb was alarmed at the intensity of Judge Farrell's animosity towards him. Not until this moment did he realize how much damage the gossip about his weekend sail had done to his reputation. That there would be retribution, he had no doubt. The only question in his mind was whether the retribution would arrive in the form of death by a thousand cuts or by a swift thrust of the sword from over the fireplace in the den.

For fear of being accused of eavesdropping, Gibb stepped outside onto the front steps and into the refreshing evening air. It was a balmy July night. The stars were shining brightly. Under more favorable circumstances, an evening such as this spent in Alicia's company would have sent his spirits soaring. Instead, he felt completely deflated. A few minutes later, Alicia joined him. Taking Gibb by the arm, she walked with him back to where his car was parked.

"Father had no business treating you the way he did."

"It shouldn't have come as a surprise. After all, you are his daughter—and you are wearing an engagement ring—and this is an old fashioned town."

Alicia drew back from him. She seemed to regard his last remark as a rebuke. Gibb walked around to the driver's side and got behind the wheel of his car. Resting her hands on the window frame, Alicia leaned towards him through the open window.

"I'm over twenty-one and I don't give a damn about this town or any of the narrow-minded people in it."

"What do you want from me?"

"I haven't figured that out yet."

Gibb put the key in the ignition and started the engine.

"When you do," said Gibb, before backing up and driving away. "Be sure and send me a text message."

Chapter

14

Hard as Gibb tried, he was unable to overcome the animosity his weekend sail with Alicia continued to generate among the townspeople. Nothing he said or did succeeded in quieting the rumor mill, not even his having alerted Art Donovan about the recent weekend he spent in New York with Piper Wilcox. Nor did the fact that Alicia had stopped taking computer lessons—or the fact that his communications with her were confined to occasional telephone calls. Computer sales were at a standstill. Even worse, his best contacts in the town and county government offices were ignoring his voicemail messages, a sure sign that serious trouble was afoot. Particularly galling was the loss of a large order for PCs the Superintendent of Schools had promised to award him.

By mid-August, the Big Byte's in-store volume had plummeted to the point where Gibb was convinced that a boycott was underway. He felt he had no choice other than to launch a major sales campaign directed at companies located outside of his territory and unlikely to be influenced by events in Chatham. At first, George the Third remained uncharacteristically silent. Ten days after the launch, the counterattack began. From that day forward, not a day passed without Gibb receiving a voicemail message from George the Third on his cellular phone. Because he was convinced that the failure to achieve his sales quota for the month of August was a greater danger to his career than was defying his Regional Manager, Gibb placed every one of his infrequent return calls during the evening hours when he was certain George the Third would be unavailable to receive them. At Corporate, the General Manager's refusal to interfere was causing ripples within the organization among the group of traditional executives who shared George the Third's slavish adherence to the dictates of the company manual.

The week before Labor Day, word began circulating up and down Main Street that Josh Bingham was due to return home for the Commodore's Ball. The Commodore's Ball was the single most important event of the Yacht Club's summer social season and invitations were much sought after. Everyone was expecting Alicia and Josh to announce their wedding plans during the ball's opening ceremony. Gerry warned Gibb that if he did anything to interfere with the wedding announcement he would be roped and blindfolded and driven out of town in the back of a pickup truck.

In the middle of the week, Art Donovan knocked on Gibb's office door at closing time. Looking more haggard than usual, he surprised Gibb by inviting him to the Chatham Beach Hotel for a drink.

"I thought you boycotted that place in the summertime."

Art frowned.

"I'm making an exception in your case."

"Sounds serious."

"I'll explain when we get there."

Gibb gathered up his sales records and jammed them into a desk draw. Art waited for him in his taxi. Gibb closed the office and bounded into the passenger's seat. Art drove off to the hotel, quietly cursing the early evening traffic clogging Main Street. Gibb sat with his hands in his lap, silently wondering what bad news Art was withholding from him.

The hotel parking lot was overflowing with cars. The overflow was backed up along both sides of the road to the town beach. Inside the hotel, the bar area was jammed with summer patrons. Mark Hogan had the music turned up louder than in the off-season. Cliques of single men and women posed for each other's cell phone cameras, conversing in loud voices punctuated by bursts of laughter. The scene was noisier than Gibb ever could remember.

Mark Hogan registered surprise when he saw Art. He signaled for a tall college age cocktail waitress to find Art and Gibb a table near the windows. The cocktail waitress was dressed in a green polo shirt and khaki shorts. Beyond the bar crowd, Gibb noticed Smitty piling plates and glasses on a tray in the middle of the room. Gibb elected not to disturb him.

The cocktail waitress led Gibb and Art to a two-seater beside the windows. Handing each of them a menu, she took their orders for draft beer. Neither of them recognized any of the patrons. Art waited until their mugs of beer arrived before delivering the bad news to Gibb.

"Gerry must have told you they're boycotting you," said Art, tipping his straw hat to the back of his head and reaching for his beer mug.

"The latest sales reports were all I needed to see."

Art leaned forward on his elbows, his hands clasped together over his beer mug, his tattoos looking more faded than usual. Gibb felt queasy, wondering what to expect next.

"Take it from me, kid—this is as nice a town as you're liable to see anywhere—"

Gibb interrupted Art.

"I know what you're about to say—it's just that people are old fashioned and set in their ways."

For the first time that evening, Art smiled.

"You took the words right out of my mouth."

"Spare me the *descendents of the Mayflower* speech—will you Art? It's been a long week."

Art rubbed the tattoo on his forearm.

"I suppose you've heard Josh Jr.'s comin' home this weekend."

"So he can take Alicia to the Commodore's Ball."

"Gerry musta told yuh."

"She heard it from Alicia's mother last Sunday after Mass."

"Maybe this will take the heat off you."

"Are you talking about the boycott?"

"I'm talkin' about the Chief tellin' Mark Hogan Old Man Bingham called Boston and told your boss he'd better yank you outta here, before business gets so bad they'll have tuh shut the store down."

"Shit, Art! Could it get any worse?"

"Not unless they were to transfer your ass to Afghanistan."

Smitty approached their table. His cap had fallen down over his forehead and his white busboy's jacket was covered with food stains. He acted overjoyed at seeing Gibb in the hotel again.

"P-O-S-I-T-I-V-E!" he shouted out letter by letter like a high school cheerleader. "Spells *positive.* Right, Mr. Gibb?"

Before Gibb could respond, the occupants of four surrounding tables burst out laughing. Gibb was expecting catcalls to follow. Instead, the patrons gave Smitty a hearty round of applause.

"Atta boy, Smitty!" someone from the group yelled.

The cocktail waitress came up behind Smitty and hugged him to her waist. Smitty smiled like he used to smile whenever Sally Kilgore was around.

"How am I doin', Mr. Gibb?" Smitty asked, expectantly.

Gibb engaged Smitty in the brother's handclasp.

"Outstanding!" said Gibb.

September brought an early chill. It was a sign that the leaves would soon be turning colors. Gibb was seated at his desk unhappily pouring over his disappointing August sales report, wondering how long it would be before corporate headquarters started badgering him about laying people off. Morale was lower than ever. He could sense it every time he wandered out to the front of the store. Except for a few customers purchasing supplies, John and Darryl had not seen a serious sales prospect in over a week.

Gerry popped into Gibb's office, announcing she thought John and Darryl should be circulating around town making cold calls, instead of staring at computer screens, playing video games. Gibb didn't believe cold calls could counter a boycott. He was certain the only two things capable of bringing about a truce were either a wedding announcement from the Farrells or a change of managers, and he was hoping the first event would occur before the second one was forced upon him.

"Josh Jr.'s back in town," said Gerry, toying with the paperclip holder on Gibb's desk. "Alicia's mother told me he's been in New Haven all week working on the Law Review. He'll be in Chatham on Saturday afternoon—in case you were planning to challenge him to a duel."

"Some sense of humor you have."

"You're running out of time."

"To end the boycott?"

"To take Alicia away from Josh Jr., dummy. Her mother says they're going to announce their wedding date at the ball on Saturday night. Once she's in that Yale Law School cocoon with him, I'm guessing the odds of you peeling her away will be about zero."

"All I can say is—they'll make a handsome couple."

"You really are a coward."

"As the saying goes—*'better a live coward'*—"

On Sunday morning, Gibb was on the road in his running suit later than usual. He was approaching the Catholic Church from the opposite side of the street when the eight o'clock Mass began letting out. Alicia and Josh Jr. were among the first people to descend the front steps. Pretending not to see them, Gibb lowered his head, faced in the opposite direction, and picked up his pace. While passing the front of the church, Alicia called out to him.

"Gibb Quinn! Come and say hello to Josh."

Gibb came to a gradual halt and circled back to the side of the street where Alicia and Josh Jr. were standing. When face-to-face, Gibb and Josh Jr. exchanged half-hearted greetings.

"You'll be happy to know we've finally set our wedding date," said Alicia, taking Josh's arm.

"Congratulations!" said Gibb. "The whole town's been waiting for this announcement."

Josh seemed to be wondering whether or not Gibb was being facetious.

"Any chance you could join us for lunch today?" Alicia asked.

Gibb looked at his watch. The thought flashed across his mind that there wasn't a chance in hell of his willingly consenting to join the two of them for lunch. He paused, mentally sorting through his standard list of excuses, searching for one that would offend Alicia the least. Alicia folded her arms, waiting for him to answer.

"I'd love to, but we're taking inventory today," said Gibb a moment later. "And I'm already late."

From the look on Alicia's face, Gibb was certain she knew he was lying. Josh seemed greatly relieved. He smiled at Gibb.

"Business comes first," he said to Gibb. "Especially when one's business is rumored to be in trouble."

Gibb was tempted to say that the Big Byte's business would be in a lot better shape, if the Binghams would quit supporting the boycott. Instead, he merely grimaced and ran off, waving goodbye to them over his shoulder.

"I hear you're quite a sailor," Josh Jr. called after him in the same sarcastic voice.

Chapter

15

The announcement that Alicia and Josh Jr. were to be married at Christmastime produced self-satisfied smiles on the faces of merchants up and down Main Street. Unfortunately for the Big Byte store's employees, the announcement did nothing to improve sales. Orders from Collingswood III to cut expenses to the bone—orders that despite Gibb's best efforts corporate headquarters refused to countermand—forced Gibb to terminate one of his salesmen. After a long, unhappy discussion with Gerry, he selected Darryl.

Darryl's termination caused morale to plummet. When John heard the news, he went into mourning, time and again declaring aloud how hard jobs were to come by in Connecticut and how unfair it was that his best friend Darryl was being forced onto the unemploy-ment roles. Painfully aware of the store's plummeting revenue stream, the entire staff had been counting on the start of Alicia's law school classes to open back up the spigot, increasing the local traffic flow enough to avoid any layoffs. Gibb had kept to himself how many promises he had to make to avoid also having to ter-minate Gerry. By then, Gibb had fully complied with Collingswood III's order to cut expenses to the bone. The service rep was reduced to working part-time. Gone were the rental car and the delivery boy and the carry-out meals Gibb was used to providing on nights when the staff was working late.

In the midst of all the doom and gloom, Alicia stopped by the store to inform Gibb that at the end of the week she would be moving her things to New Haven. As a parting gesture, she asked whether he was interested in joining her that evening for a movie and for a bite to eat, afterwards. Gerry was standing on the opposite side of the checkout counter from Alicia, looking like she had just received a death threat. For his part, Gibb was beyond caring whether an evening out with Alicia could make matters worse for the Big Byte. Thinking it might be his last chance to say goodbye to her, he accepted her invitation. Alicia agreed to pick him up at his apart-ment in time to make the seven o'clock movie.

While driving Gibb back to Hampton Court, Gerry announced that for the first time in her life she was seri-ously considering leaving Chatham. What was it about Gibb that brought to the surface all of townspeople's mean-spiritedness, she wondered aloud. Their behav-ior was so un-Christian, she was having great difficulty

JOHN HENRY BREBBIA **197**

understanding how the townspeople could act this way and continue to fill the churches on Sunday. She felt terribly let down by people she had known all her life. Without a doubt, the town had lost its virtue. She came to this dispiriting conclusion with tears streaming down her cheeks. It had left her feeling worse than a jilted lover.

Gibb worried about Gerry the same way he would have worried about a sister, if he had a sister. Despite being bitterly disappointed, he doubted she would leave Chatham while her mother was still alive. Glancing sideways at her sagging chin, he pictured her hope of finding someone to love her other than her mother fading farther into the distance than her career at Big Byte.

"Your problem is, you spend too goddamn much time taking care of everyone else," said Gibb, "and not enough time taking care of yourself."

"Spoken like a true Christian."

"Trust me—pretty soon this crap will all blow over. And what you need to start thinking seriously about, is getting back into shape. You've got to get rid of the negativity."

"What did you have in mind?"

"You could start by taking aerobic classes and getting serious about your diet."

"What good would that do?"

"I've been around enough to know that somewhere out there—maybe in Boston, or Hartford, or New Haven or New York—there's the right guy for a terrific person like you. But you'll never get to meet him, if you sit around eating junk food and feeling sorry for yourself."

"It's easy for you to say—when you've *never* had any trouble finding a date."

"All I'm saying is—attitude has a lot to do with it—and you need to change yours."

"I suppose this is your idea of tough love."

Gibb laughed.

"Call it what you want. In situations like the one you're in, a little self-help goes a long way."

✿ ✿ ✿

Gibb was splashing cologne on his face and in the bathroom mirror examining his flannel shirt and khakis. Above the sounds of the local rock station, he heard Alicia honking the horn of her BMW convertible. Snatching his windbreaker from the bedroom closet, he dashed for the front door. Before stepping outside, he checked the side pockets of the windbreaker for his house key. Reminded that he had forgotten his rolls of dimes, he dashed back to the bedroom. The rolls of dimes were on the top of his dresser where last he had left them. He grabbed them and stuffed them into the side pockets of his windbreaker. At the sound of Alicia leaning on the horn, again, he dashed for the front door. This time, he hurried down the front walk to the parking space where Alicia was waiting for him with the top up and the motor running.

The movie let out at nine o'clock. Afterwards, Alicia suggested they go to the hotel for hamburgers and beer. By the time they arrived, only four cars were left in the parking lot. Alicia parked her car in a space near the side entrance. Patches of fog drifted in off the beach, giving the hotel a desolate, after-the-season look. The summertime army had withdrawn, taking with it all of the summer season's noise and excitement. Such was the way with resort towns everywhere, Gibb was thinking, while holding the side door open for Alicia.

When Gibb appeared from behind Alicia, Mark Hogan looked like he had seen a ghost. Gibb guided Alicia to the same window table where he and Art Donovan had their last conversation. In the entire dining room, there were only six other patrons. The bar was populated by empty stools.

In response to a shout from Mark Hogan, a middle-aged waitress emerged from the kitchen. The waitress was not anyone Gibb had ever seen before. She took their order for hamburgers and mugs of draught beer. Gibb fell into the habit of the townies, talking to Alicia about the new waitress as if she were an intruder. Alicia joked about what a year in Chatham had done to him. Gibb was saddened, thinking about the time twelve months before when he had first met Sally Kilgore. He felt guilty not having called the state hospital for a report. Silenced by his feelings of guilt, he sat still, staring out the window at the waves washing over the beach.

Alicia laid a hand on his wrist, reclaiming his attention. She started describing her plans for the fall semester. Before she was finished, the waitress reappeared with their hamburgers and mugs of beer and set them down in front of them. They proceeded to eat and talk.

"What happens after law school?" Gibb asked.

"The Public Defender's office in New York or San Francisco—I hope. It depends on where Josh decides to locate."

"I thought you wanted to be a prosecutor."

"I've decided I'd rather be on the side of people who can't afford a criminal defense lawyer."

"It's hard for me to picture Josh Bingham working in the Public Defender's office."

"Don't be silly. Josh is a star. With him it has to be the biggest and best firm in New York or San Francisco. He expects to be the youngest associate ever to make partner."

"Doesn't sound like you'll be able to spend a lot of time together?"

Alicia put down the remains of her hamburger. Her face was flushed. She folded her hands in her lap. In the background, Mark Hogan had substituted tunes from bygone eras for the rock 'n' roll CDs the proprietor forced him to feature during the summer nights.

"In the big leagues, sacrifices are the price you pay for success," said Alicia in an irritated manner. "Besides, its quality time that counts—or haven't you heard?"

"It's a little too programmed for me. Or maybe I'm just jealous."

"Jealous of what?"

"Of people who know exactly what they want out of life. But I suppose none of this matters—as long as you're sure Josh is the right guy for you."

Alicia was taken aback.

"Of course he is! Why else do you think we've been dating for five years?"

Gibb was thinking of what Alicia seemed to have in mind that night on the forward deck of the Happy Ending before Uncle Tom interrupted her.

"As far as I'm concerned—this just proves you're loyal to each other—it doesn't necessarily mean you're in love with him."

"What do you mean?" Alicia asked. "Everyone of our friends thinks we're a perfect match. We have so much in common. We both love the law—we come from similar backgrounds—our parents have known each other since we were born—they get along great. What else matters?"

"Nothing. I guess. If you're talking about a merger deal. When it comes to marriage, doesn't romance play a part?"

"Since when is an escapee from *the war zone* an expert on marriage?" Alicia asked, testily.

"You've got me there."

"I suppose you think I should be seeing shooting stars and walking into walls?"

"Something like that."

Alicia paused. She seemed to be thinking hard about what she should say next. Gibb leaned back in his chair, worrying that he had offended her.

"It can't all be candlelight and violins," Alicia said, earnestly. "With all the career pressures, there has to be a solid foundation—otherwise you wind up in divorce court."

"Maybe so—but boredom has ruined a lot of marriages."

Alicia was incensed.

"Josh is not boring!"

"That depends on your definition."

Alicia's eyes narrowed. She took a sip of beer and stared at Gibb. Gibb thought she might get up and walk out on him. In the long pause that followed, he found himself again staring out the window at the waves washing over the beach, worrying about what Alicia might say next.

"Why did you turn me down for the Fourth of July dance?" Alicia asked with sadness in her eyes.

"I was afraid of losing all my customers."

"Spoken like a true romantic."

"If I'd lost all my customers, I wouldn't have had any excuse for staying in town. Besides, what difference does it make?"

"More than you'll ever know."

The waitress reappeared and cleared off their plates. She began walking away.

"Where's Smitty?" Gibb called after her.

"Business has been really slow tonight. Mark let him off early."

The sound system went silent momentarily. When the music resumed, Bunny Berrigan's rendition of *I Can't Get Started* filled the room.

"I've never heard this song before," said Alicia. "Where do you suppose Mark got it."

"From me. It's a 1940s Bunny Berrigan recording. I came across it in a music store in Greenwich Village."

Gibb had chosen not to tell Alicia the whole story about how he happened to acquire the Bunny Berrigan recording. The truth was, being a devotee of music from the 1940s and 1950s, Tim Perkins had directed Gibb to the music store in Greenwich Village in search of the

Berrigan CD. At the time, Tim told Gibb he thought the lyrics described to perfection Gibb's relationship with Alicia Farrell. That was why Gibb had decided to buy it for Mike.

"Who's Bunny Berrigan?"

"Only the greatest trumpet player that ever lived."

Alicia was listening to the music, intently.

"I can relate to that," said she.

"To the fact that Bunny Berrigan is the greatest trumpet player that ever lived?"

"No. To the '*I can't get started*' part."

Alicia took both of Gibb's hands in hers. She leaned over and pressed her forehead against his. They stared directly into each other's eyes. Unable to seize the moment, Gibb pulled back and raised his beer mug.

"Here's to the Belle of Chatham Township—and much as it kills me to say it—to a marriage that lasts forever."

They finished their beers and left the bar. Mark Hogan waved goodnight to them. Gibb reached the bottom of the stairs ahead of Alicia. He pushed open the side door and stopped so suddenly, Alicia bumped into him. Reaching behind him with his right hand, he held Alicia back.

"Something wrong?" Alicia asked.

"Smitty's in trouble," said Gibb in an anxious voice. "Go back upstairs and tell Mark to call the police."

Alicia hurried back up the stairs.

Gibb's attention was fastened on Mel Price and Mel's biker friends, the same three hoodlums that had threatened to beat him up the morning Art Donovan came to his rescue. Clad in their black leather biker uniforms, the four of them were formed in a semicircle in front of their big black Harleys at the end of the hotel parking lot nearest to the beach. Smitty was kneeling down in front of the burly one they called Animal. Animal was wearing studded boots and a red and white polka dot bandana tied around his forehead. In the light from the lone street lamp, Gibb could see his bare stomach protruding from under his black shirt. Animal was swigging from a bottle wrapped in a brown paper bag. With his free hand he unzipped his fly and pulled out his penis. Every muscle in Gibb's body tensed.

Gibb quietly closed the door behind him. Stepping out into the darkness, he proceeded towards the group at a dead run. His heart was pounding so loudly, he imagined he was hearing drums. None of the bikers noticed him approaching. They were focused on what Animal was threatening to do to Smitty.

"Let him up," Gibb shouted from ten yards away.

Mel was standing a few feet to the left of Animal. The bikers called Gonzo and Slim were standing to the right of Animal. From their appearance, Gibb assumed the four of them were stoned.

Mel turned around and shouted back at Gibb in slurred speech.

"Not until he sucks Animal off."

Gibb's hands were jammed into his windbreaker pockets, squeezing his rolls of dimes. He brushed past Mel and extended a hand to Smitty. From the look on Smitty's face, it was obvious to Gibb that he was in fear of his life.

Smitty was so panicked, he stuttered when he spoke.

"Please, Mr. Gibb," he said, laboriously. "Don't let them hurt me."

Mel grabbed Gibb by the arm and spun him around. "Get lost cowboy," said he menacingly.

Gibb reacted instinctively. Reaching into his windbreaker pockets, he grabbed for his rolls of dimes. With his left and right fists, he unleashed vicious, lightening-like blows at Mel's face. The punches landed with such force, they broke Mel's jaw. Mel staggered out of the way, moaning loudly. Animal dove at Gibb head first. Gibb kicked Animal in the groin so hard Animal's forward motion was momentarily arrested. Locking his hands together in a ball, Gibb brought them down on the back of Animal's neck and with a knee to his chest sent him sprawling backwards over his bike. The bike crashed to the ground, bringing the other bikes down with it.

Out of the corner of his eye, Gibb saw the glint of a chromium wrench descending towards his head. He responded by driving his left fist into Gonzo's stomach. The force of the blow caused Gonzo to double over. Gibb hammered at Gonzo's nose with his right hand, breaking Gonzo's nose in several places and splattering blood all over Smitty's busboy's jacket. The scene was one of carnage.

Sounds from a police siren kept Slim from using his tire chain on Gibb's head. Slim dropped the tire chain and helped Animal to his bike. The two of them roared out of the parking lot and off into the night, in their haste almost sideswiping Chief Nickerson's police cruiser. Mel and Gonzo were left sprawled on the pavement, groaning loudly.

The police cruiser came to a stop a short distance from Mel and Gonzo's overturned bikes. Out of the police cruiser bounded Chief Nickerson. He charged forward between the beams of the police cruiser's headlights, his *Glock 19* drawn, his potbelly shaking. Gibb knelt down beside Smitty. Placing an arm around his shoulder, he held him tightly. Chief Nickerson stood over Mel and Gonzo, pointing the gun at them.

"I don't suppose either of you would be interested in pressing charges?" said he, sarcastically.

"Son of a bitch busted my jaw," said Mel.

Chief Nickerson turned to Gibb.

"See that you're down at headquarters first thing tomorrow morning."

From out of the darkness, Alicia appeared.

"If he is, Uncle Tom will be with him," said she to the chief in an angry voice. "And they'll be the ones pressing charges."

Chief Nickerson whirled around and reached under Mel's armpits, pulling him to his feet.

"I'm taking you two over to County Hospital for X-rays," he said to Mel and Gonzo. Turning towards Gibb, he pointed a finger at him. "Just make sure you're at the Big Byte in the morning."

Alicia and Gibb waited while Chief Nickerson helped Mel and Gonzo into the back seat of his cruiser. Gonzo was holding a kerchief to his bleeding nose. After the police cruiser departed, Alicia and Gibb escorted Smitty around to the help's quarters.

Smitty did not stop shaking until they got him to the top of the wooden stairs leading to his room above the hotel garage. Alicia held his hand and escorted him inside. She turned on the overhead light. The yellowed bulb gave off a dull glow. With one arm around his shoulder, she walked Smitty over to the metal cot in the far corner of the room and sat him down. The bare room was damp and cold. It had the look of an abandoned Army barracks. Gibb removed Smitty's sneakers and told him to lie down. Alicia spread the blanket over Smitty, tucking it under his chin to keep him warm.

"They comin' back?" Smitty asked Gibb.

"Not in your lifetime."

Alicia placed a hand on Smitty's forehead.

"Go to sleep now. Gibb won't let anyone hurt you."

Smitty closed his eyes. Quietly moving to the door, Alicia switched off the light. Gibb followed close behind her. Alicia opened the door. She stepped outside. Gibb was backing out the door when Smitty sat straight up and called out to him in an anxious voice.

"They were tough—tough as they could be—weren't they Mr. Gibb?"

"Not tough enough," said Gibb matter-of-factly, before closing the door.

Alicia drove away from the hotel. Gibb was certain that she intended taking him directly home. She surprised him by turning the car north in the direction of the Yacht Club access road.

"Isn't it a little late for a sail?" Gibb asked, jokingly.

Alicia did not answer him. She continued past the turnoff to the Yacht Club access road. A short distance later, she turned the car into a dirt road Gibb was not aware existed. The BMW's headlights shone on a small wooden sign nailed to a tree by the side of the dirt road. On the sign were painted the words: *Private Road—Do*

Not Enter! The dirt road led to a sprawling two story Victorian house overlooking a cove. The house had weathered shingles. A wide veranda extended along both sides. Alicia brought the car to a stop beside the front walk and switched off the engine. Parallel rows of blue hydrangeas pointed the way to the front door. Gibb sat motionless, wondering why Alicia had brought him to this secluded spot.

"What are we doing here?"

"This place belongs to an aunt of mine," said Alicia, fishing in her purse for a set of house keys. "She spends most of her time in the South of France. This is where I come, whenever I need to be alone."

"Where does that leave me?"

"I'll explain when we're inside."

Gibb followed Alicia up the front walk and into a world of wicker furniture and print fabrics. Alicia took Gibb by the hand. She led him on a quick tour of the downstairs. The house was spotless and comfortable-looking throughout. To Gibb, it wreaked of *old money*. The tour ended at the bottom of the front staircase. Alicia placed a foot on the first stair. Again taking Gibb's hand, she tugged on it.

"Come on. I want you to see the upstairs."

Gibb had no idea what was happening. His heart was pounding almost as hard as when confronting Mel Price and his hoodlum friends. Alicia led him to the top landing, then down the hallway to the room at the end. Gibb felt like he was in a trance.

The end room was a spacious bedroom, featuring a large bay window overlooking a small sandy beach. The beach was situated in the middle of the cove. Rimmed with tall pine trees, the cove's smooth surface shimmered in the moonlight. A queen size bed was positioned against the wall facing outward towards the bay window. Gibb thought to himself that anyone resting on the bed would have a full view of the open ocean lying beyond the cove. The scene was tailor made for a romantic encounter.

"Isn't this beautiful," said Alicia, gesturing towards the whitecaps coursing through the entrance to the cove.

Before Gibb could respond, she stripped down to her bra and bikini panties and climbed under the covers. Gibb was dumfounded. This was the last thing he expected from the one girl whom he had not even managed to kiss goodnight. He pictured himself being led by Judge Farrell and Josh Bingham Sr. to a tall tree and lynched by a mob of outraged townspeople. In a state of partial paralysis, he eased himself over to the end of the bed, where he stood motionless before Alicia, awaiting instructions.

Cupping both hands over her mouth, Alicia imitated Uncle Tom's command voice.

"Now hear this! This is your captain speaking—I'm ordering you to disrobe immediately!"

Gibb struggled to maintain his composure. As casually as he knew how, he stripped down to his shorts and placed his clothes on the cedar chest pushed up against the end of the bed. Alicia stared at his muscular body. Hesitantly, Gibb began moving around to the opposite side of the bed from where Alicia was lying with her head propped up on a pillow. She stopped him with an outstretched hand.

"Before you get into bed, I want you to drop your shorts and stand at attention," said she in a husky voice.

Gibb did as instructed. Standing there before Alicia completely naked, he was hoping he looked to her like a shadowy imitation of Michelangelo's statue of David. Alicia stared at him for a long moment. He began to shiver.

"Well?" he asked.

"I've always wondered what a gladiator looked like in the buff. You can come to bed now."

Gibb reached under the covers and climbed into bed beside her. They melted into an embrace so tight and so hot, they had to push back the covers to cool down. Drawing apart, they lay side by side, holding hands.

"I forgot to mention—I have a rule against making love to engaged girls," said Gibb, at last.

"I'm not a girl. I'm a woman."

"A woman who's on the pill—I hope."

Alicia sat up against her pillow with her hands behind her neck.

"Guess again."

Gibb reached over and placed his arm around her neck, gently drawing her to him. He stared out the bay window at the ocean.

"I can't believe you survived four years at a place like Yale and now you're willing to play Russian roulette."

"I didn't think of it as a big moral issue. I just made up my mind I wasn't going to be like most of the other Yalie women I was hanging out with. Then in my sophomore year my roommate contracted herpes from a guy she was dating at Harvard. That settled it—besides, I figured someone who'd been around as much as you have would be prepared."

"Ordinarily, you'd be right. Only in your case, I assumed it would be a total waste of time."

Alicia rolled over onto Gibb's chest and kissed him on the lips.

"Then we'll just have to take our chances—because this is definitely my last night as the *Virgin Princess.*"

Chapter

16

Gibb took his time getting to the Big Byte the next morning. His knuckles were sore and his right shoulder felt like it had been dislocated during the melee in the hotel parking lot. The store was as empty as it had been for the past few weeks. Chief Nickerson was waiting for him at the checkout counter. He was drinking coffee from a Styrofoam cup, bantering with Janet. John and Gerry busied themselves straightening out the display cases. Gibb approached Chief Nickerson, suggesting they repair to the privacy of his office. Chief Nickerson picked up his service cap and followed Gibb.

Gibb ushered Chief Nickerson into his office. Chief Nickerson positioned himself with one foot resting on the seat of Gibb's extra chair. Gibb sat behind his desk, facing the chief. Filling both cheeks with air, the chief exhaled in an exaggerated manner, looking as though he intended to read Gibb his rights.

"Do I need to hire a lawyer?" Gibb asked.

"Not this time. Mel and his hoodlum friends aren't in any position to press charges."

Gibb was relieved.

"Then what's the problem?"

"You're the problem."

"I was only trying to keep Smitty from being molested."

The chief folded his arms across his chest and rolled his eyes towards the ceiling in exasperation. Seconds later, he pointed a finger in Gibb's face. Gibb pushed his chair back against the wall and rubbed his sore shoulder. The chief's eyes narrowed.

"Only reason why people have put up with you this long is 'cause they don't want Gerry going on unemployment. Then you have to break it off by putting the town stud out of commission and getting some of his horny clients so worked up they're after me to book you for assault and battery and put your ass behind bars."

"Mel's the one who belongs behind bars—and you know it."

"It took a lot of guts to do what you did for Smitty last night," said the chief in a friendlier tone of voice. "But don't expect any thanks for it. The powers that be still want you run out of town. And the sooner the better—if you get my drift."

"What happens, if I refuse to leave?"

For the second time, the chief directed an exasperated look at the ceiling. His breathing was labored. He seemed to be deciding whether or not he should say to Gibb what he was about to say. Gibb prepared himself for the worst.

"That would be a very stupid move. Gerry tells me your big boss thinks you're the greatest computer sales-man that ever lived. So take this dumb cop's advice and go on back to the West Coast while the going is good. That way, you won't have to spend the rest of your life trying to explain away your trailer park days in Las Vegas—or that rap sheet you left behind."

Gibb was visibly shocked at hearing that the Chief of Police was aware of his rap sheet. It dredged up painful memories of the violent past he had worked so hard to put behind him when he left Las Vegas for good.

"Hey!" said Gibb, excitedly. "I was there when the judge ordered those juvenile records sealed."

"Not to Judge Farrell, they weren't."

The chief dropped his foot to the floor and started to leave Gibb's office. He bumped head first into Gerry. Gerry linked arms with him.

"Caught any desperados lately?" she asked jokingly.

The chief threw his head back. Feigning anger, he puckered his lips.

"What would you know about desperados? To you, they're all God's children."

Gerry's look turned serious.

"Not if you're referring to those animals that tried to sodomize Smitty."

The chief jerked his head in Gibb's direction.

"Do everyone in this town a favor and try wizing up your boss—before it's too late."

The chief unlocked his arm and disappeared from view. Gerry stepped inside Gibb's office. She closed the door. Gibb remained seated, rubbing his knuckles.

"You've got this town in an uproar again."

"What was I supposed to do? Let those animals have Smitty?"

"Of course not! But I've never heard such wild rumors. They're saying your father's a mobster and that you were run out of Las Vegas by the sheriff."

"Give me a break!"

"There's more—you're supposed to have saved Alicia from being raped last night and this is why she's fallen madly in love with you and is about to break her engagement."

"Shit!" said Gibb. "A rumor like that could be the final nail in the coffin."

Janet interrupted Gibb, saying there was a telephone call for him on line 1—from corporate headquarters. Gibb grabbed the receiver and whipped it to his ear. The voice on the other end asked Gibb to please hold for the General Manager. A moment later, the General Manager came on the line.

"Things seem to be getting out of hand," said the General Manager, sternly.

Gibb's stomach started to churn. He was panicked, thinking that somehow the latest news about his personal problems had filtered back to Seattle by way of George the Third.

"I don't follow you," said Gibb, with maximum apprehension.

"I've been looking at the August numbers. Your store is back on the endangered list. Is there something else we should talk about?"

Gibb was relieved that the GM was unaware of how much influence Gibb's personal problems had on the final August sales figures. Yet he assumed it would only be a matter of time before news of his personal problems reached his patron.

"Not that *I'm* aware of. What do you advise me to do?"

"Now that you've paid your dues, I've recommended you for an exec slot that's about to open up in Seattle. You have twenty-four hours to make up your mind— after that, you're on your own."

More dejected than ever, Gibb said goodbye to his patron and buried his face in his hands. Gerry moved around behind him. She began massaging his shoulders.

"More bad news?"

"That was my patron. He's given me until tomorrow to decide whether or not to transfer back to Seattle."

"What happens, if you turn him down?"

Gibb drew an imaginary knife across his throat.

"What are you going to do?"

"I'm thinking maybe it's time to fold my hand."

For the next two hours, Gibb sat at his desk worrying that his situation was spinning out of control. He decided to call Tim Perkins for advice. At 9:00 a.m., Pacific Standard Time, he dialed Tim's office telephone number. Tim answered on the first ring.

"I'm in trouble," said Gibb.

"Tell me what's wrong this time—and don't leave out any of the details."

Tim listened patiently to Gibb's description of the events that had transpired since he returned from his sailing trip with Alicia. Having heard Gibb out, Tim zeroed in on the town's visceral reaction to the news that Gibb and Alicia had spent an overnight on her uncle's yacht. In his opinion, the level of animosity directed at Gibb was entirely predictable. Without waiting for Gibb to process this piece of wisdom, Tim launched into his standard lecture about the suffocating attitudes of people in small New England towns and about the odds being 1000 to 1 against Gibb ever being able to change those attitudes—no matter how much success he achieved in the world of business.

"You know how much I hate to admit defeat," said Gibb.

Tim fell silent for a moment. When he resumed speaking, it was in an impatient voice.

"Do you remember the last scene from *Death of a Salesman?*"

"The one where his neighbor said that Willy Loman was '*a man way out there in the blue, riding on a smile and a shoe shine.*' No one who heard that line could ever forget it. What's your point?"

"My point is—Chatham has robbed you of your smile *and* your shoeshine—"

"And?"

"It's time to call it quits and come home to Seattle where people are a lot more interested in what you've accomplished in life than where you came from or how much money your father has."

Gibb felt the latter sentiment was a bit disingenuous, considering how much money the Perkins family had accumulated over the years and how big a part it was known to have played in their becoming pillars of the Seattle community. Yet he found it impossible to argue with Tim's logic. Coming as it did from the person Gibb trusted the most, this is what convinced him to stage an immediate strategic withdrawal back to the West Coast.

Gibb called his patron back and accepted his offer on the condition that Gerry be promoted to store manager. The General Manager capitulated. Afterwards, Gibb felt that a great weight had been lifted from his shoulders.

He remained at the office long past closing time, cleaning out his desk and organizing his files and writing and rewriting a note to Gerry. Included with the note was a check for $3,000 made out to Gerry. Finally, when his briefcase was packed and he was ready to leave the office, he placed the note in an envelope and sealed it. The note was brief.

Gerry,

I never did learn how to say goodbye. The money is to take care of Smitty. I'm counting on you to continue giving him computer lessons and to buy him a warm winter coat. The GM has agreed to promote you to store manager. Tomorrow morning, you'll receive an email from headquarters giving you your instructions. Call me on my cell next week and I'll fill you in on my promotion. The best news is that now you also have a patron to protect you from George the Third. Make sure you do whatever it takes to keep from letting the GM down.

Your friend for life,

Gibb
PS. I meant what I said about the right guy for you being out there.

Art picked Gibb up and drove him back to his apartment. Along the way, Alicia called him twice on his cellular phone. He let both calls go to voicemail. When he arrived home, two more voicemail messages from Alicia awaited him on his landline. Intending to ring down the curtain on Chatham, he ignored both of them.

✪ ✪ ✪

At 6:30 a.m. the following morning, Gibb was seated in the front seat of Art Donovan's taxi. He was wearing his windbreaker and his khaki pants and his hiking boots—the same outfit he wore when first he arrived in Chatham. The weather was overcast and blustery. Art looked at Gibb in the rearview mirror.

"I feel like I'm drivin' a getaway car."

"You're not far off," said Gibb.

"Believe me. You're doin' the right thing."

"Then how come something that's supposed to be so right makes me feel so bad."

"Best thing you can do is forget yuh ever heard of this place."

The taxi entered the train station parking lot. It came to a stop opposite the staircase leading to the platform.

"Sometimes the seven o'clock is late. Want me to wait with yuh?"

"That won't be necessary."

Gibb handed Art the fare and two $100 bills.

"A two hundred dollar tip?"

"For all the free rides," said Gibb.

Art tipped his straw hat back on his head.

"You know, I can't take this from yuh."

"Sure you can."

Art smiled broadly.

"On second thought, maybe you're right. I can use it to buy the Regulars a couple of rounds of the good stuff—on you. They'll like that."

Gibb got out of the taxi. He retrieved his baggage from the back seat and walked around to the driver's side. Art rolled down the window and leaned his head out.

"I gotta hand it to yuh," said he, slowly shaking his head up and down. "You're the only one ever managed to scare the livin' shit outta the powers that be—and that's sayin' a hell of a lot."

Gibb banged on the hood. He watched while Art saluted and backed away. Art seemed older to Gibb— older and more resigned—like a father who was seeing a son off to war.

At a few minutes before seven o'clock, Gibb was alone on the railroad platform, stomping his feet to keep his blood circulating. His bags were on the platform along-side him. His look was forlorn. He was lamenting the loss of Alicia and the turn of events that forced him to leave town like a prison escapee on the lam.

The sound of high heels clicking on the metal stair-case leading to the platform broke his concentration. Alicia appeared on the top step opposite the place where he was standing. You can run but you can't hide, thought Gibb, watching her sprint towards him. She was dressed in a business suit and she looked more desirable than ever. In what seemed to him like a flash, she was standing in front of him, placing both hands on his shoulders. Tears were streaming down her cheeks.

"How could you leave without telling me?"

"I'm really lousy at saying goodbye."

Alicia removed her hands from his shoulders and reached into the pockets of his windbreaker, seeking to warm them. She withdrew his rolls of dimes and squeezed them.

"So this is how you were able to take on the four of them," she said, as if fitting the last piece into a puzzle.

"One of the tricks I learned in *the war zone*."

Alicia returned the rolls of dimes to Gibb's pockets. She threw her arms around his neck, drawing him closer to her.

"Are you sure you have to go?"

Gibb withdrew her arms. He took her hands in his.

"I'm afraid we're both out of choices."

"Uncle Tom can take care of Caleb, if that's what's worrying you."

"It's not just the chief—it's the whole damn town!"

Alicia stepped back a few paces.

"Don't you get it?" she asked, slowly shaking her head from side to side. "I'm trying to tell you that I love you."

A train whistle sounded in the distance, silencing both of them. Alicia reached out for Gibb. They poured themselves into an embrace.

"Uncle Tom and Mary are getting married," Alicia whispered in Gibb's ear.

Gibb pulled back and gave Alicia the thumbs up sign.

"We could make it a double wedding."

"Refugees from *the war zone* make terrible husbands."

"After last night, I feel like I've been in *the war zone* with you."

"You're not making it any easier for me."

The train rumbled onto the platform. Alicia stepped backwards, wiping tears from her eyes.

"I could have you arrested for stealing my heart."

"All aboard!" shouted the conductor.

Gibb unzipped his windbreaker. He reached into his shirt pocket for a small pad of paper and a ball point pen. Hastily, he scribbled a note and pressed it into Alicia's hand. Alicia read it aloud to herself.

Come New Year's Eve—if you still feel the same way—meet me at the Fairmont Hotel in SF - Suite #412

Gibb handed his baggage to the porter and boarded the train. The train started off. Gibb stood on the steps, waving to Alicia. She looked up at him and shouted—"*Is there something special about the suite number?*"

Gibb shouted back at her.

"It's in the old section!"

END

11234889R00137

Made in the USA
Charleston, SC
09 February 2012